OTHER YEARLING BOOKS YOU WILL ENJOY

THE FAIRY REBEL, *Lynne Reid Banks*

THE FARTHEST-AWAY MOUNTAIN, *Lynne Reid Banks*

FEATHER BOY, *Nicky Singer*

SPARKS, *Graham McNamee*

THE HERO, *Ron Woods*

THE QUIGLEYS, *Simon Mason*

JUNEBUG IN TROUBLE, *Alice Mead*

Lynne Reid Banks

I, Houdini

{ the autobiography of a self-educated hamster }

Illustrated by Terry Riley

A YEARLING BOOK

Visit us on the Web! www.randomhouse.com/kids

Educators and librarians, for a variety of teaching tools, visit us at
www.randomhouse.com/teachers

ISBN: 978-0-440-41924-2

Reprinted by arrangement with Delacorte Press

Printed in the United States of America

November 2003

15

Happy Valley Elementary
3855 Happy Valley Road
Lafayette, CA 94549

To Adiel $\left\{ \text{Mark} \right\}$,

Gillon $\left\{ \text{Adam} \right\}$,

and Omri $\left\{ \text{Guy} \right\}$

And to Valerie and

all at "Hicklebee's"

I am Houdini.

No, no, no. Not that one—of course not. He's dead long ago. Besides, he was a human being and I am a hamster. But let me assure you that, as my namesake was no ordinary man, I am no ordinary animal.

Well, that much is fairly obvious, isn't it? I mean, what ordinary hamster even knows he's a hamster? What ordinary hamster can think, reason, observe—in a word, educate himself? Show me the hamster, anywhere, with an intellect, a vocabulary like mine! You can't. Nor can you show me one that can live with humans on a footing of absolute equality because he can understand their language, and because, quite frankly, he has more brains in his head than most of them have.

I fear you will think me conceited. I assure you I'm not. It's merely that I have a just and objective appreciation of my own exceptional qualities. It would be as futile to deny that I am exceptional as it would be for an ordinary hamster to boast that he was my equal.

Besides, if I were conceited, I would claim to be perfect. I don't. Certainly not! I have my faults and weaknesses, my moments of frailty. I, too, have made mistakes, succumbed to temptations. But I think I may fairly claim to have built up my character, over the months of my long life, until not many fingers could be pointed at me in accusation. Indisputably I conduct myself with more wisdom, ingenuity, and restraint than many of the humans I see about me—not that that's saying much.

Here, then, is the story of my life so far. From it you may judge if I am not, in truth, as extraordinary in my ways as the Great Houdini was in his.

My birth and infancy are almost lost in the mists of memory. I think I may have begun life in a pet shop. It was certainly a large, cold, airy place, exceedingly smelly. Every now and then I catch a whiff that carries me back to those dimly remembered early days—when a friend of my family brings a dog to the house, for instance, and once when I met a mouse, which I shall tell about in its turn.

At all events it was not a bad place, and I remember I had companions of my own kind there, who gave me warmth by day when we all cuddled up together to sleep.

It's strange that, when I think now about living with other hamsters, I shudder with horror at the idea. With one exception I have never seen another hamster since I became mature. And believe me, I never want to. If I ever did see one, I believe I would be overcome with rage, and fly to attack it. Why this should be, I don't know, for I have a very calm temper as a rule, and despise those who lose their self-control (something I see all too often in this house, I regret to say). So, whatever I have to complain of in my life, it is not loneliness. I am never lonely.

My worst trial here was imprisonment. I say "was" because

luckily it happens less and less now. The Father is my worst enemy in this respect. He has very fixed ideas about "pets" (as I suppose I must laughingly call myself, taking the human point of view). "Pets are all right in *their place*," he keeps *on* saying. (He does tend to repeat things, a sign of a small mind.) His notion of my place is, of course, my cage, and wherever and whenever he catches me, he grabs me up and stuffs me back through that dreaded little entrance tunnel and claps in the round stopper. He never seems to believe it when the boys tell him I've even found a way round *that*.

Anyway, it doesn't worry me too much anymore. The Mother, or one of the children, will soon take pity on me if I just go about it the right way, if I can't get out by myself. So I just whip up the tubes into my loft, unearth something tasty from my store, and then curl up and go to sleep. I must say it's quite cozy up there since they put the bits of flannel shirt in, though I much prefer my nest under the kitchen floor. One does tend to prefer a home of one's own choice, arranged and decorated to suit oneself.

Here I go, rambling on about the present when I really meant to tell the story of my life. I just wanted to make it crystal clear that I am—well, shall we say, rather unusual? Rambling has always been one of my weaknesses. I just have to follow my nose wherever it takes me—and some fine scrapes it's led me into, I must say!

Well, so I am, as I say, a rather extraordinary and quite exceptional "little furry animal," as some people call anything smaller than a pony that runs around on four legs and can't actually talk. I call *them* large hairless animals, and I try to use, in my thought, the same degree of superiority that humans do about us. I must admit that nothing infuriates me more than being treated as a pet, picked up, stroked (usually the wrong

3

way), made to climb or jump or run or whatever it is my supposed owners want—and as for eating from their hands and all that sort of degrading nonsense, I've not time for it.

Mind you, my protest against this sort of thing is, nowadays, limited to trying to avoid it by escaping, which is my specialty (hence my name). I wouldn't dream of biting, which I regard as very uncivilized behavior. "Brain, not brawn" is my motto. Besides, they're so vulnerable with their bare skins, it's not really sporting when you've got jaws and teeth like mine. I won't say I've never bitten anyone, but the feeling of shame I had after letting myself go was awful, not to mention the disgusting taste. . . .

Anyway, as I said, I was bought (it sounds so quaint!) from wherever-it-was and brought here at an early age. I wasn't half the size I am now, and of course, I was entirely ignorant. I didn't even know that I was a hamster, let alone a golden one—I learned that from listening to the children, whose speech I soon picked up just by keeping my ears open.

At first I was too agitated to learn anything, however. I well remember my first night here. They put me into a deep cardboard box with some water and grain in separate bowls. I don't suppose they meant to keep me there.

They hadn't bought a cage yet, which was silly of them, because inside ten minutes I had discovered that my claws could get quite an easy grip on the roughish sides of the box, provided I used the corner to give myself purchase as I climbed. It took three or four attempts, but I am nothing if not persevering and I was soon hanging over the top. It looked rather a long way to the floor (amazing, when I think of the heights I can jump now!), but even then I was no coward, and half jumped, half slithered down the outside, headfirst.

I was in a large, open area, which I now know like the back of

4

my paw, but which was a whole unknown world to me then. Like the idiot I am *not, as a rule*, I hadn't stored any of the grain in my cheeks before leaving the box, and now that I was free, I could have done with a morsel of something, but it was too late to think of that. Escape was then, as now, my main objective, and I was about to sample my first taste of real freedom.

The area was a room that the Father uses as a kind of workshop. Apart from the kitchen, where my nest is, I think it's now my favorite room in the house, because it is so beautifully untidy. It is full of things to explore and wonderful places to hide, and I spent the rest of that night doing both to my heart's content. You must remember, I'd never been free before, and I'm certain that this first blissful taste of it was what gave me my lifelong passion for escape, concealment, and exploration.

I climbed into toolboxes and under heaps of sacking, clambered up a big soft mountain that turned out to be a battered armchair, and fell off into a wastepaper basket (fortunately wicker—those smooth-sided metal ones are death traps to me). I ran behind huge bits of furniture and took a quick nap under a lovely warm radiator (after foolishly trying to climb up it and burning my paws. I was always very wary of sources of heat after that).

I made several attempts to climb the telephone wire, and got so exasperated because I couldn't that I eventually chewed it right through. I chewed quite a lot of other things as well. I didn't know any better in those days, or for quite a while afterward, to tell the truth. I'm afraid those teeth of mine, with their constant need of being worn down lest they grow through my skin, led me to be very destructive when I was young. I've often made excuses for the Father's intolerant attitude to me because of this. But of course I didn't know anything about destructiveness then. When I saw something chewable, I just chewed, and I

chewed a fair amount that first night, I can tell you. Apart from anything else, I was trying to find something to eat.

Eventually the obvious solution occurred to me. I went back to the box. It wasn't hard to find, even in that vast area, because of the delicious smells of food and water pouring over the top of it. I didn't think I could climb back into it because the corners were the wrong sort from outside, but I walked round it and found they'd carelessly left it standing against a pile of telephone directories. Of course I was up these like a flight of steps, plopped back into the box, had a long drink, and stuffed my cheeks till they would hold no more. It was a lot harder to climb out with all that load weighing me down, but determination won the day and soon I was safe and warm under the radiator, having a good feast before settling down for my day's well-earned sleep.

Well, I didn't sleep long, needless to say. I had hardly dozed off before an appalling hullabaloo broke out in the vicinity of my abandoned box.

"He's gone! Goldy's gone!" shrieked Guy, who was then only five. He'd come to say good morning to me before going to school and, finding me gone, fell into an uproar. Floods of tears, wails, and cries—dear me, it was all very unpleasant and deplorable. I knew nothing about the modern child in those days and was both alarmed and shocked. (I seem to remember now that my Mother used to nip us if we so much as squeaked. Perhaps that's why I hardly ever utter a sound.)

His two brothers, Mark and Adam (as I later learned were their names), came running in, followed by the Mother. A search was put in hand, and I would have been speedily found if I had not scurried off, keeping to the wall, which was luckily blocked in by furniture for most of its length, to a tailor-made hiding place I had noted the night before. I had not chosen it for

7

my day nest for two reasons. One, I hadn't known I was in any danger, so security had not seemed more important than warmth and comfort. Two, it was dirty. I never liked the smell of dust, and I am fastidious, so I have never ventured into dirty places except in an emergency. But this was one—I could see the Mother's feet bearing down on me across the wooden floor—so I just slipped through a hole in the baseboard and found myself in a drafty dark cave.

Instinct told me I was now perfectly safe. There were so many places I could have been concealed that, to the boys' rage and dismay, the Mother soon told them that the hunt was hopeless. They were bundled off to school, bitterly complaining, and Guy still, alas, in tears. Later in my life I gained enough sensibility to feel uneasy if I had made any of the children sad, but at that time I had no room in my heart for anything but selfish satisfaction that I had evaded them.

I made a rough nest for myself in the inch-deep fluff, put my nose between my back legs, and fell instantly asleep.

chapter 2

I was captured again the same night.

I had made the mistake of de-cheeking all the grain I had brought from the box, storing it under the radiator, where I had had to leave it when I ran to the hole. So when I woke up in the evening, I was starving. I remembered at once where the food was and, cautiously emerging from my hiding place, crept back along the wall to reclaim my little hoard.

It was gone.

True, I found two or three grains of wheat and one sunflower seed, which I gobbled up. There was still a strong smell of food, so I poked my nose out from under the radiator and saw a trail of grain leading temptingly off into the distance—right across the open floor. Fool that I was (then), I trotted obligingly out to collect up this trail, but was scarcely halfway along when I was pounced on.

I got the fright of my life, and I may be forgiven for trying to bite on that occasion—anyone would have done the same. But the Father (it was he who had trapped me) had a thick glove on, and my teeth were not then what they are now. Holding me firmly, he carried me some distance and then put me down.

I stopped hissing (I no longer hiss when enraged, but most primitive hamsters do—it is a danger signal) and looked around. I was in a deep plastic bin with straight, shiny walls. I didn't bother to entertain the Father, who was hanging over the top watching me, by trying to climb them—one look showed me it was useless. I simply crouched where I was, seething with fury. After a while the giant head above me vanished, and I heard his voice calling the children.

Soon their three faces were hanging above me. They were all grinning with excitement.

"How did you catch him, Daddy?" (Of course I didn't understand the actual words then, but my imagination must be allowed some rein here.)

This question, put by Adam, was followed by the Father's self-satisfied description of his brilliant coup. Meanwhile Guy's little hand crept toward me, fingers temptingly extended. The middle one, as it approached my face, was just the perfect diameter for my mouth to enclose, and it must be remembered, in mitigation of the crime I then committed, that I had just been caught and imprisoned by one too big and well-gloved for me to revenge myself on. Nevertheless it was nothing less than wicked of me to sink my teeth into that little bare fingertip and I cannot now think of it without shame.

The truly awful shriek that followed simply shattered my nerves. I think it was the noise, more than the taste, that taught me my first lesson in manners. The Mother rushed in and carried Guy off. Adam and Mark began scolding me. The commotion was terrifying. Though I couldn't then make out the exact words, I knew that everyone was angry with me, and that the

Father was threatening me. All my own anger had melted away into fear and confusion.

I cowered down, but the inside of the plastic garbage can (that was where he'd put me) offered no hiding place and I felt dreadfully exposed. Nothing is worse than having nowhere to hide. Even my eyes were hurt by the bright light, and I shut them. After a while the hubbub died down. I ventured to look up. The rim of the bin, far above me, was blank—all the faces had gone. I felt frightened and miserable. I ran around a few times and put my front paws up against those slippery unclimbable sides. No use. I crouched there, filled with a sense of hopelessness, for I had no experience to fall back on that might have told me what to expect.

I had fallen into a miserable half-sleep when something soft fell on me. Opening my eyes with a jerk of fright, I found myself covered with some light, soft stuff, which blocked off some of the light and gave me the feeling of being safe and hidden. I began at once to make a nest in it.

Once, I glanced up. The Mother was hanging over the rim, watching me. She spoke to me, but not harshly. Considering I'd recently bitten her young one, I realize now she was showing a very forgiving nature. Also an understanding one, for when her natural anger cooled, she had realized what I needed most— bedding—and had given me some paper shavings.

Some time later she brought me a dish of food and some water, but by that time I was comfortably asleep and I didn't find it till I woke up in the evening.

Evenings are always my active time. I had had a good sleep, despite my upset, and when I'd had something to eat, I felt ready for anything. And soon enough things started to happen.

Mark arrived. He was wearing gloves now, thick leather ones, though if he had but known it, there was no need for them—nothing short of a direct attack on me would have induced me to bite him. Very cautiously he reached down and, after a short chase—I was not anxious to be picked up—caught and lifted me.

Now, I have said I don't like being held—not for long periods. But I don't mind sitting in between two warm hands, well supported by the one below and gently stroked by the one above. This pleasant experience now happened to me for the first time. I was nervous, of course, and trembled a good bit, but Mark has a feeling for animals and I sensed this at once, the way one can. He put his face close to me and his warm, boy-smelling breath came over me. I don't know why, but being breathed on by a human gives one confidence, provided, of course, one does not instinctively sense danger. There was nothing menacing about Mark's breath, and his face looked kind and interested.

We stared and breathed at each other for some moments. Then I tried to get away. I always do this after being held for a short time. It's really no more than a natural restlessness. Mark endeared himself to me by understanding this. He relaxed his upper hand and let me run up his arm. He was wearing a woolen sweater that gave me ample footholds—I love climbing up rough knitted surfaces—and I was soon exploring his shoulders, poking my nose between his collar and his neck, and even sniffing around his pink ears. He wriggled and giggled. I suppose I was tickling him. After a while he lifted me down again, stroked me soothingly for a few minutes more, and then laid me gently on his knee.

Now it shouldn't be thought that I had been deliberately lulling him into a sense of false security by not trying to escape before. I was too far from the ground then, and I knew it. But now he was sitting down and I had only to make a dash headfirst down his trouser leg and I was on the floor and running like mad.

Mark dived after me, but too late. I had dashed under the frill of a sofa cover, and by the time he had lifted it to peer underneath, I was already three pieces of furniture away, crouching beneath a desk. The next thing was an upright piano, but there was quite a gap between the desk and it, and I could see Mark's shoes, turning slowly in the middle of the floor, watching for me to make a dash. I waited till the heels were toward me and then I ran. Ran! I skimmed. Mark just caught a glimpse of me and spun round, but too late! I was safely behind the piano and there was nothing he could do about it.

It was not a very well-made piano, and it was easy enough to get in through a hole in the back. The innards were fascinating, quite the most exciting playground I had ever been in. Human athletes, whom I have seen on television, have gyms to exercise in, with all sorts of apparatus. Hamsters have pianos—at least, they should all have them, if humans were understanding enough or the hamsters themselves were cunning enough to escape and find them. I would certainly recommend a good upright piano to any hamster who fancied himself as an athlete.

It was in my piano that I first learned muscle control, agility, how to fall correctly, how to swing by front and back paws, how to jump horizontally, diagonally, and vertically, and of course, how to climb. I mean really climb, where some might find the going impossible. Nothing could be more useful, believe me, in the life of an escapologist who frequently has to fend and forage for himself. If I had not trained in the piano, I doubt if I could have navigated the vegetable rack, let alone climbed up into the biscuit drawer, three shelves up in the kitchen cupboard. . . . But I must not get ahead of my story.

Well! If I had enjoyed my freedom in the Father's workroom, how much more did I enjoy the fun of my freedom in the piano! I may say that before the night was out I had thoroughly explored most of its lower half, though I was not yet skillful enough to mount to its higher regions. I was fortunate in one thing. It should have been perfectly dark in there, for how could light get in? Yet it was not. Quite a lot of light filtered down from somewhere above, as if through a window, and until the family (who had given up hunting for me) had gone to bed, switching off the lights, I was able to enjoy myself, clambering around swinging, diving, and so on, to my heart's content.

When the darkness did come, I was able to come out of the piano (I was still small and supple enough in those days to squeeze through the holes around the pedals) and give the whole living room a good going-over before bedding down in the wastepaper basket among the bits of paper and cigarette packets. I was completely hidden and felt quite safe.

Alas! The short jump I had had to make to get down into the basket from the upholstered chair had misled me—I thought in my ignorance it would be equally easy to get out. But the sides of this container were not wicker, but metal, and thus in the morning I was speedily detected because of my frantic scrabblings among the rustling papers.

Back to the bin. But I was not in despair this time. Experience had taught me that opportunities for escape would present themselves if I waited patiently. And so they did.

chapter 3

How I hated that bin! Even with the shavings, and various bits and pieces the boys put in from time to time, it was a loathsome dungeon to me. Not only could I not get out, I couldn't *see* out. There was no way to take any real exercise; nothing to play with (I was still a youngster then and needed toys) and nothing to do. No challenges. No opportunities. No amusements. Only—after that first blissful outing—hope.

I was taken out fairly frequently, once the boys realized that that one bite had been an aberration. They all became fond of me (as I of them, in a way) and liked to take me out and play with me, especially as an alternative to helping their Mother, doing their homework, or practicing the piano. (I'm sorry to say not one of them is what I'd call diligent.)

But it was not every time that I could elude them. They were obviously pretty careful after my escape from Mark. I don't blame them for that. It became clear to me from the beginning that our views and objectives were, and presumably always would be, quite different—even opposed. They regarded me as their pet, their plaything—their possession. They wanted to know where I was, to know that I was available whenever they wanted me. I knew myself to be a freedom-loving individual, belonging to no one. I wanted to be free, to live my own life in my own way. It wasn't so much that I positively objected to being fed, petted, and played with. I just knew, right from the start, that the whole business of my life was to be—escape.

The boys soon knew it too. That was why they changed my name. This happened after I'd been in the house about a week and had escaped four times. The fourth time I ran away from Adam.

Adam, who is a bit of a fibber, will tell you I bit him. Nonsense. No need. Adam is a highly imaginative child—not a coward at all, but hampered by being able to picture to himself what may happen and how certain unpleasant eventualities would hurt. Thus one only has to give a sudden jump in his hand and he will drop one like a hot brick. Sometimes it's enough to turn one's head swiftly toward his thumb, without even baring one's teeth. . . . The thing is not to do it when he is standing up, and always to be ready for the drop when he lets go.

I first tried this out when he had me in his bed one night. I think I dimly realized even then that he was disobeying his Mother when he stealthily carried me up the darkened stairway into his room. There he switched on a flashlight under the blankets and trained it on me while I scurried about in the soft, warm caves, looking, as ever, for a way out. Finally he tired of this game and scooped me up in his hand, dangling me over the edge of the bed. That was when, sensing his slight uneasiness, I tried out my little jump.

It worked splendidly. In another moment, I was on the floor— I landed quite well for a novice, rolling over once to break my fall—and the next second I was bolting for the fireplace.

What made me go for that, I don't know. In a newer sort of house (such as I spent some time in later), I would have found my way blocked by some gas or electrical barrier. But this was an old house, and the original fireplaces were still there. No fire, of course; but a grate, and the iron bars the fire is made on. I got down through a broken bar and lay in the ashy darkness while poor Adam scampered round with his flashlight, fruitlessly hunting for me. I heard him desperately whispering, "Goldy! Goldy!" My sympathy was aroused, for I knew he would get into trouble; but I was not going to let myself be "binned" again just for that.

I lay still. I'd learned that they could often locate me by sound. After a while, the poor child crept back into bed. I heard him sniffing to himself a bit. Then the flashlight went off, and all was quiet.

I quietly climbed through the gap onto the bars, and from there I made my way to the corner at the back of the fireplace. The bricks were rough and covered with old soot and cinders clinging to the wall. Just for fun, I began to climb, all my four feet outspread, clinging with all my claws. Rough surface or not, it was sheer. Up and up I climbed, until I found myself on a little sloping ledge. I didn't realize I was right up inside the chimney. I could feel cold air coming down, and by looking up, I could see vast distances into a starry sky. I'd never seen Outdoors before, even through a window. It frightened me—yes. But it intrigued me too.

I couldn't sleep on this ledge, and I didn't fancy climbing any higher, so I slid down again into the grate. Then I began to explore the room.

Young as I was, I knew where the entrance to the room was because of the draft of air blowing under the door. I knew that through there lay absolute freedom. I snuffled the length of the draft and, finding a crack that led upward, decided that was the place to chew. I settled down to it. The carpet was easy and I soon had a pile, almost as big as myself, of red fluff heaped around me. Finding this didn't open the door, I began on the wood of the door itself.

A grown-up would have woken at the gnawing noise I was making, but Adam slept placidly on, snoring slightly. It was lovely to gnaw. I hadn't realized the joy of it till I really got down to it. I loved the feeling of the hard, resistant wood, gradually being worn away by my teeth, and wearing the teeth away at the same time—something that must happen if my teeth, which grow all the time, are not to grow right through my cheeks and lips. I had no notion, of course, that I was doing anything wrong. I gnawed until I had quite forgotten what I was trying to do. The gnawing became an end in itself.

At last I sensed that morning was coming. I was healthily and happily tired—and frightfully thirsty, of course. I could smell water in the room and soon traced it to its source. It was on a wooden chair beside Adam's bed. That chair was no easy matter to climb, for its legs were smooth and it had only one bar. Four or five times I fell back before I finally made it to the seat, but there was my reward—a mug of water. It was too tall for me to drink out of easily, so I stood erect and put my front paws onto the rim.

In another moment I was on the floor, soaked to the skin.

It gave me a fright, I can tell you. Of course I know better now than to tip a full mug of water over myself. And I hadn't even had a drink! Luckily Adam sleeps like a log. Despite the clatter he just grunted, rolled over—and silence fell once more; so I was able to creep back to the leg of the chair and drink as much as I liked from the little trickle that was still pouring from above like a hamster-sized waterfall.

Feeling, despite my few blunders, quite satisfied with my night's work, I now returned to the grate and made myself a scratch nest among the ancient ashes, which were remarkably snug and comfortable. I could have done with some protection overhead when full daylight came, and I can't say I slept well. In any case I was soon woken by the most fearful hullabaloo. This was because Mark had found I was not in the bin. Suspicion at once fell on Guy (suspicion always tends to fall on Guy because he's naturally mischievous), but Adam, though, as I've said, not an entirely truthful boy, was not one to stand by and see his little brother falsely accused. I'm pleased to say he owned up. After that the entire family descended on his room—and then the real ruckus began.

I had already picked up some of their speech, so I can give more or less verbatim the scene that followed.

"Crumbs, what's all this mess by the door?"

"Look at the carpet! He's gnawed it right to the backing!"

"Never mind the damn carpet—" (This was the Father, fairly roaring with rage.) "Look what it's done to the wood!" (The Father always, I found, referred to me as "it.") "Wasn't it enough that we had to spend a fortune getting the telephone wire replaced? Are we going to have to have new carpets and new doors all over the house?"

"Adam, how could you?" (The Mother, very reproachful.)

Adam began boo-hooing. "I only wanted to play with him—"

"So why did you let him go, stupid?" This was Mark, very superior.

Then came the lie direct. Well, I don't blame him. He was on the spot, poor boy. "He bit me and I dropped him!"

"Let me see the place," said the Mother, instantly concerned.

"Yeah, let's see it—if it's there," said Mark in quite a different tone.

"It—it healed in the night."

"Huh! A likely tale," said the Father. "Now you children listen to me! That wretched little house wrecker (he meant me!) is to be found, caught, and put in the bin. Furthermore, it is to stay there until a cage can be bought for it."

"Fanny's giving us a proper hamster cage for Christmas," said Guy. Fanny, I was to learn, was their grandmother.

I'd been trying to ignore the whole row and get to sleep till that point, but now I pricked up my ears. I didn't like the word "cage" one bit. Still . . . it had to be better than that vile bin.

"CHRISTMAS!" yelled the Father. "That's three weeks away! The little beast (me again!) will bring the whole house down around our ears if we don't do something about it before then!"

"Maybe we could ask Fanny to give it to us now."

"Good. Do that. Buy it today. But meanwhile nothing—no playing, no television, *no food*—until that thing's been caught and incarcerated in the bin where I can keep an eye on it!"

Well!

There wasn't much option for me after that but to scuttle across the floor and let them catch me. Very self-sacrificing of me, wasn't it? Still, knowing that a proper home was in the offing, and that in all probability my stay in the bin that day would be my last, I decided to be decent and spare the poor kids the useless agony of hunting for me.

I was rewarded for my noble action with the most ear-splitting shouts the moment they saw me. If only hamsters could cover their ears!

"Holy Mackerel! Look at him!"

"He's not golden anymore—he's black!"

I hadn't stopped to think what I must look like. All my fur was stained with soot and thick with ashes. The water had just made me look more filthy and bedraggled. Of course I should have taken time to clean myself before settling down to sleep. It was another useful lesson for me, and never since have I let a day pass without giving myself a thorough licking and grooming.

Mark was holding me in his hands and scolding me.

"You bad, bad hamster!"

I stared at him defiantly.

"We can't call you Goldy anymore. You're not worthy of such a nice name."

"I know what we ought to call it," said the Father grumpily as he went out. "Housebreaker."

"No," said the Mother. "I know! Let's call him after the great escapologist—Houdini."

And that's how I got my true name. And when I found out about my namesake, believe me I was proud of it.

chapter 4

Of course, the children wanted to know all about Houdini, and so did I, as you may imagine. The Mother put them off for the moment, but that night, when they were ready for bed, she told them about him like a story. Fortunately I had given them the slip again by then and was under Guy's bed (a nice low one, with a frilly thing right to the floor, which he hates but I love) and heard all about my namesake.

Houdini, in case you don't know, was a magician who began by doing conjuring tricks and ended up as the most famous escapologist of all time. An escapologist, of course, is someone whose profession is escaping. It's an act, like an act in a circus or on the stage. Houdini's helpers would tie him up tight with ropes, chains, handcuffs, and so on; then they'd put him in a thick sack that they'd fasten at the neck; after that they'd wrap more chains around the sack, padlock them, and then—if you can believe it—they'd often hang him up by the *feet* a couple of yards off the ground. Then they'd give him the old "ready, steady, go," the drums would roll, and in a matter of a few minutes somehow or other he'd have wriggled free. Don't ask me how. Nobody ever really knew his secret. Of course he must have had flexible bones, and joints that would bend backward, and he had a few obvious tricks like swelling himself up while they were tying him so the knots wouldn't be so tight. Still, there was more to it than that—more than anyone ever found out.

Naturally it was hard for me to understand all this at the time. I hadn't then watched all the television and seen all the pictures that I have now, which meant I really didn't have a clue about handcuffs, chains, etc. But I realized that this human had been world-famous for the very thing I had already decided to dedicate my life to. I shuddered at the idea of being tied up or dangled in midair, and hoped nothing so terrible would ever happen to me; but I determined then and there that no matter what challenges faced me in the future, even those, I would try to overcome them. After all, I had one priceless advantage over the human Houdini. I had rodent teeth. Ropes would be nothing to me. And when it came to flexible bones, and being able to make oneself look bigger and then squirm through places you'd think a snake couldn't get through . . . I was ready to bet I could hold my own in that respect with the greatest escapologist ever.

I was able to prove this, and a great deal more, very soon.

My new home arrived the following day. The boys came charging into the house with cries of "Where's Houdini? We've got his cage." But I was nowhere to be found, having, as I mentioned, got away the previous evening. I was, in point of fact, exploring a new room—Mark's—and when I heard them tramping about looking for me, I dived into a very small hole I'd noticed earlier in the floor by the fireplace. I swear a fairly large mouse might have got stuck in it, but I made myself into the merest thread of my former self and in a moment I found myself huddled in the deep dust between the joists.

These are long planks standing on edge that you'll find between the floor of an upstairs room and the ceiling of a downstairs room. Between them are long spaces, roadways to
someone my size, and as there were plenty of places where I
could climb over the tops of the joists, I had what then seemed
like a huge playground.

For a while I rejoiced. They would never catch me now! How
could they? There was only the one way in, and not even a child
could get his hand through that! Happily and, I fear, smugly, I
made a nest in a very warm corner near where I had come in
(I like a bit of light). I did wonder at the time just why it was so
warm; I didn't have the experience to realize that that thick,
long, hot thing nearby was a hot-water pipe. It was much too
hot to touch, but it gave off enough warmth to make me comfortable and sleepy. I curled up and dropped off, not feeling the
least bit guilty about the row that was going on about me overhead.

I woke up feeling distinctly uncomfortable. To begin with,
the heat had increased to a point where I had dreamed I was being roasted alive. I jumped up hastily and moved to a cooler
spot. There was no light coming through the hole now, I noticed, so I decided that it would be perfectly safe to pop up and
attend to my other discomfort—hunger.

I hadn't managed to eat much the day before, what with one
thing and another; that's the trouble with escaping upstairs—
there's very little food lying about, and I hadn't yet thought
of leaving stores hidden in various strategic places all over
the house. I realized I'd probably have to go downstairs to forage. I'd already seen the stairs, while being carried up and
down them; they were thickly carpeted and I felt sure I could
manage them all right, though getting back up might be a bit of
an effort.

I returned to the spot, below the hole, where I had been sleeping. It was awful just standing there, right next to that pipe—if hamsters could sweat, I'd have been wringing wet. I looked upward. I could just about see the hole. I stood up on my back legs, idiotically convinced that if I stretched to my fullest height, I would somehow miraculously find myself climbing out. But alas! The hole was a good two or three times my height above me.

When I realized this, I didn't lose my head—at least, not until I had explored every possibility. I climbed onto the top edge of the nearest joist and ran to and fro, but it didn't pass near enough to the hole. The only thing that did was that wretched hot pipe. I could see an easy way onto that, farther along, and once on top of it nothing could be simpler than to run to the hole and climb out—it passed just nicely under it. But who could stand on a thing like that? Even standing near it I felt my fur was scorching.

Now I did begin to panic. I'm ashamed to admit I felt really sick with fear. How would I ever get out? How would I live if I had to stay in here? My nose had already told me there wasn't so much as a moldy bread crumb anywhere in the large space between the floors, where I now grimly realized I was trapped. As for water! Not a drop, of course. And wasn't I beginning to be thirsty, what with the heat and my growing terror!

A grown-up hamster who's got himself into a mess will, if he's got any sense, at once sit down, partly to conserve energy and partly to think. I behaved ridiculously. I ran around in circles. I made funny little noises that I hadn't known I could make. I climbed up on the joist and fell off it again. I even tried to climb the pipe, and I hurt my paws, of course. Oh, that pipe! It was maddening to see the way it lay, just beneath the hole, offering the perfect escape route, and yet—impossible to use.

At last I was fairly worn out. I couldn't sleep—I was too distracted—but I did lie down, at some distance from the hole, and just stared at it in misery. I supposed I would just waste away there in the dusty dark, slowly starve to death, and be found, perhaps, years later, a moldering skeleton. If hamsters could weep, I would have wept, with frustration, fear, and self-pity, though of course I'd brought it all on myself.

Morning came. A ray of light fell through the hole. I heard Mark moving about above me. And suddenly I knew what to do.

When I'd escaped before, I had often been caught when accidentally or carelessly making a noise. Hamsters have no proper voice, as I've said, though they can utter faint squeaks and hisses; but their feet scrabbling on a hard surface draw attention to them. Now I had to draw Mark's attention. But how? It wasn't so easy in that hot death trap I'd landed myself in. The floor was thick with dust and I could walk there without a sound. The joists were the same. The pipe was metal and I could have made a terrific noise on that, but . . . So what was I to do? In a flash of genius it came to me.

What I had to do was—gnaw.

I climbed up on the joist nearest to the hole, and set to work. I made as much noise about it as I could. I got my mouth full of dust and cobwebs and sawdust. Never mind! I ground my teeth against the wood, ignoring my terrible thirst and weariness. Gnaw, gnaw, gnaw!

It worked! After a very few minutes, I heard Mark stop moving. Then I heard his footsteps coming nearer. I gnawed feverishly! The next thing I knew, the ray of light went out. I stopped working for a moment and looked up. Peering down into the darkness was—an eye.

I squeaked.

The next moment he was up and running. "Mom! Mom! Houdini's under the floorboards!"

My heart gave a great leap! At least they knew where I was. Getting me out, though, proved to be another matter.

All five of them were soon crouched above me. A flashlight was shone into the hole. I stood in its beam on my hind legs and positively begged like a dog. I heard the children going "Oooh" and "Aaah" and the Mother said, "How on earth can we get him out? Poor little thing!" I felt a poor thing too, and longed to yell up at them, "Never mind the sympathy, what about a drink?" Would they never think how thirsty I must be after a night in that fearful heat?

"Well," said the Father slowly, "you'd better give it some water."

Bless the man! I forgave him a great deal, past and future, for that.

How to give me a drink was the next problem. First a strange little spout came down through the hole. This turned out to be the special bottle that had come with the cage, which you drink from by sucking, but of course I couldn't reach it. Next they poured a little trickle of water down and I managed to catch a bit of that before it sank without a trace into the dust, but it wasn't much good. Finally they lowered a tiny container on a bit of string. I think it was a bottle lid. Most of its contents spilled before it got to me, but I lost no time in putting away the rest of it.

Then I was ready for a meal, and it wasn't long coming. They poured enough grain and bits and pieces down there to bury me. In fact, that's just about what they did—I was eating the first lot when somebody poured down a new lot on top of me! In the meantime they were discussing what to do.

"We'll have to take the floorboards up," said Mark.

"Oh no," said the Father. "That means taking the carpet up and goodness knows what. He got down there; he can get up again."

"But he can't, Daddy! It's too far down!"

A beam of light and an eye appeared at the hole and there was a long, exploring pause. Finally the Father said, "He could easily climb out from the water pipe."

"It's too hot for him to stand on!"

"Oh Lord," said the Father. "You know what that means, don't you? We'll have to turn everything off and let it cool down."

And that's what they did. Poor things, they all went without heat and without hot water for some hours and eventually the pipe grew cold and I was able to hop up onto it, run along the top to the hole, and—I was out!

What a relief. Indescribable!

Of course I was pounced on the moment I got my head out, but I didn't care. I was just so glad to be above ground again, to see daylight and to get away from that hateful trap. Do you know that at that moment, when they picked me up, petted me, scolded me, and popped me into my new cage, I honestly thought I would never want to escape again?

chapter 5

I must describe my cage in some detail so that you'll understand my brilliance in finding a way out of it. Of course it was designed for ordinary hamsters, not for me. Still, I heard Adam remark that the man in the shop had said it was escape-proof, so I can't help feeling rather proud that it wasn't proof against me.

I call it a cage, but that suggests something with bars or wire rather like a box. It was nothing like that. It was round and in layers, like one cake pan on top of another. The two main sections of it were joined, in a very clever way, by a plastic tube, just the right diameter for me to climb up and down through it. It took me just two minutes to discover I could do this by bracing my back against the inside and using my feet. Above the second "cake pan" was a third, much smaller, known as a "loft," joined in the same way with a climbing tube. That was my sleeping place.

In the bottom section, the ground floor so to speak, was a built-in wheel for me to exercise on. As soon as I'd had a quick

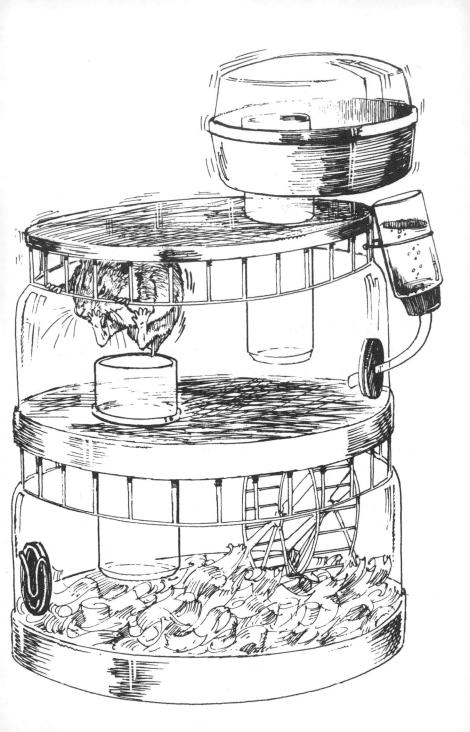

look around the whole premises, I hopped onto this wheel to have a go. It was fun. You just run and run; the faster you run, the faster the wheel turns, so you're always right way up. I could soon do it so fast that Adam exclaimed, "He's just a blur, I can't see the spokes anymore!" Of course, I soon discovered that the wheel is nothing but a substitute for running free from place to place, at least that was the makers' intention; but as I have seldom had to use it except for pleasure and exercise, I've never grown to hate it.

The floors of the place were made of some solid stuff, but the walls were clear plastic. Near the top of each layer of plastic were little bars. This was to let air in. By standing erect I could put my nose through these bars.

There was only one official entrance. On the ground floor there was a round plastic plug, which, when pulled out from outside, left a hole. It was the way to freedom—the only way I could see at first. The loft had a sort of lid that could be taken off, but it fit very tightly. There was one other hole, through which my water spout was stuck. All in all, not a bad little place as cages go, but none too promising for a dedicated escapologist like me.

Well, they put some food in for me, and some bedding, and the water spout, and they watched me for ages till I'd finished exploring and then off they went. I was pretty well whacked, so I went up into the loft, carrying the bedding with me, made a nest, stored some food underneath it, had a drink, and went to sleep. In my dreams I was already exploring ways to get out. I gnawed the metal bars and they fell away like matchsticks. Of course when I woke up, I realized they wouldn't, but I had a try just to make sure. As I gnawed them, my nose was outside the cage, and I could smell all the fascinating smells of the house. I had to get out! But I was not impatient. Even the human

Houdini couldn't have escaped from his chains and sacks without practice and cunning.

Well, in brief, I was in that cage for several weeks. True, they let me out occasionally to play with me, but you can't think how careful they were—their Father had threatened that I would be taken back to the shop if they let me escape them again. One thing they did, though, was to put me at the top of the stairs and let me climb down. There was no question of escape—Mark stood at the top and Adam and Guy at the bottom—but I didn't mind. It was wonderful experience, and great fun too, plopping down those stairs headfirst, one by one. Halfway down I stopped and tried going back up again. As I'd suspected, it was harder, but the carpet gave my claws excellent grip and I was at the top again before the boys recovered from their amazement. Goodness me, how excited they were! They called their Mother and made me do my stair trick over and over again until I was quite worn out. I didn't really mind. I just practiced doing it faster and faster. I knew it would come in useful one day.

My hamster house was kept on the upstairs landing, outside Mark's bedroom door. It wasn't the quietest place for it. The first time the Mother ran her vacuum cleaner along the strip of carpet alongside me I woke up with such a jump I nearly popped the lid clear off the loft! And the boys, playing in their rooms, made a terrible din. So did their parents, shouting at them morning and night to get them either out of or into bed. However, there was a certain period of each day when I could count on peace and quiet. Then I could sleep or, when I was awake, do a bit of serious thinking.

What I thought about most was how I was going to escape.

By this time I'd tried everything, from chewing the plastic to pushing out the plug. The first was no good because there were no edges I could get a start on with my teeth—all the rims were bound with metal. The second I couldn't manage—the plugs were jammed in and secured with wire springs. For a long time, the problem defeated me. But at last I found the answer—by accident.

One night, when I'd been cooped up for three days without them taking me out for a run, I became really desperate. I was so restless that I really felt life wasn't worth living if I couldn't stretch my legs properly. I'd run on that idiotic wheel until I should have been exhausted, but I wasn't. It just made me all the hungrier for freedom.

I've mentioned that when I grow desperate I sometimes do silly things, like running round in circles in the bottom of the bin or going down into that awful hole. Well, now I did something silly too. I tried to climb out through the bars. This was quite mad of me really, because they were only an inch high and about half an inch apart and the whole thing was lunacy, but— well, I felt crazy, as I said, so I got hold of one bar in my teeth, grabbed hold of two others with my front paws, and just— struggled. Scrambling upward with my back feet, pressing my shoulders against the ceiling, I strained and pushed, *willing* those bars to give way and let me through. Naturally, they didn't—but something else did.

Suddenly I felt something give. It wasn't the bars; it was the solid ceiling above my head! I paused, wondering if it was another dream, and then, with redoubled energy, strained again. I was not wrong! The whole top of the house was shifting, tube, loft, and all!

Heaving and struggling, I pressed upward with my back. The trouble was there was no foothold for my paws, or I could have moved the silly lid in a minute. As it was, it was a slow, laborious business; but in the end, I'd shifted it just enough for me to wriggle through. Then, head down, I jumped. In another moment I was heading for the stairs.

Oh, it was wonderful to be free! I scampered down those steps in a twinkling. A feeling of almost hysterical delight came over me as I saw that all the doors downstairs were open. Lights were out—everyone had gone to bed—but it wasn't too dark to see my way, and there were plenty of smells to guide me. I headed for the living room first, the piano room I call it. I was so over-joyed to get back into my piano again! I hadn't realized till then that I had grown—I was now full-sized—and to my excitement I found I could now climb right to the top inside. There was a marvelous place there, with rows of little wooden hammer things with their tips covered in lovely soft felt. Ah, I thought. Perfect for a nest! I'd already planned during my weeks of im-prisonment how I would make nests all over the house to re-treat to if I ever got the chance, and stock them with food so that no matter what room I was in, I would have a safe refuge where I could stay for some days.

I got to work on the felts. As soon as I had chewed off enough soft stuff to fill both cheeks I would nip down to a platform I had found about halfway to the ground, de-cheek the bedding, and then climb up to get more. I did the better part of the whole nest before I allowed myself time off to forage for a bite to eat.

I thought I'd have to go to the kitchen for that, but there was a really delicious smell right there in the living room, which I de-cided to investigate first. I traced it to the area of the fireplace. It was coming down from above somewhere—a fresh, fruity smell, richer and moister than grain. I was determined to find out what it was, and get some, if it was any good. But how to get up there?

After several head-on attempts, which the still-glowing em-bers foiled, I went to the side of the fireplace. There I found a perfect way up. Mind you, I won't say it was easy. It was a straight wall, with a sticking-out bit covered with rough stuff like brick or cement; but the wall, luckily for me, was covered with some material like sacking. This gave me all the foothold I needed, and feet spread, I was up that angle as quickly as I went up my tubes at home. Pretty soon I was on the mantelpiece above the fire, and there I found my prize.

It was a large vase full of sprays of red berries. I'd never tasted a berry before, but I had had fresh fruit and salad, so I knew it would be good. I scrambled up the wall, pressing my back against the vase, and pretty soon I was having a marvelous time swinging on the sturdy branches and twigs, gobbling up these little red berries until neither my stomach nor my cheeks could hold any more.

I was just turning my thoughts—not without some worries—to the much more difficult downward climb, when I spotted a particularly luscious-looking bunch of berries right out on the tip of the branch I was on. Yes, it was sheer greed that made me go for them—I don't deny it. I just couldn't bear to leave them there. Also, perhaps my antics in the piano and on the stairs had made me too confident. None too cautiously I began to edge along the branch toward the cluster. . . .

Need I go on? With the added weight of the berries in my cheeks, I was too heavy. The branch, the berries, the vase, and I were all soon lying in a puddle of water in the hearth, the air around still echoing with the crash the vase made as it broke.

Well, I thought, picking myself up with a dainty shake of my wet fur, at least that solves the problem of getting down. But there was another problem now, because the noise had woken the Father, who could already be heard thumping about upstairs. Houdini, said I to myself, this is no place for you! Quick as a wink, I scurried behind the piano and up into my brand-new nest.

The fights about the telephone wire and the carpet and the

door were nothing compared to what followed my escapade on the mantelpiece. The Father seemed to go completely mad. He literally jumped up and down, purple in the face with rage. (How do I know? I'll tell you. There was a little window in my piano—actually a little sliding-glass panel. Don't ask me why, but it was extremely useful, as I could sit on the hammers in a shadow and peep out at what was going on in the living room. That was where the light came from, inside.) He did more than threaten now—he issued ultimatums. "No more chances!" he bellowed. "Back it goes! That, or I'll kill it—I will—I'll kill it with my bare hands!"

Yes, very intemperate of him, wasn't it? And all that was before he'd discovered what needless to say I had not known—that all that soft stuff I chewed off the little wooden hammers prevented a number of notes from playing on the piano.

He went to the lengths of pulling the piano out from the wall, taking its back off, and hunting for me through all the works. My nest was demolished, of course, and my store of berries was stolen. But fortunately for me, by that time I was no longer there. I had found my favorite place under the kitchen floor.

chapter 6

My luck seemed to be with me altogether, so far as that kitchen was concerned.

It was not one of your shining modern affairs with all the gadgets, stoves, washing machines, and so forth set so tightly side by side that even a mouse couldn't squeeze between them—no. It was your old-fashioned, half-converted kind, with huge chasms between and behind the bits of equipment. I could safely run right under the stove, for instance, and one of the cabinets—the one that turned out to contain my beloved cookie drawer—had no back. The drawer itself, three shelves up, was not quite backless, but its back was half broken so that, having swung up to it, it was a simple matter to climb in and help myself. The children's visits to that drawer left it in such chaos that it was a long time before the Mother realized that most of the crumbs, torn wrappings, etc., were my work.

Well! So on my very first exploration of this domestic paradise, I discovered a hole in a corner of the floor under the sink.

You may imagine I was exceedingly careful not to go down into it until I had checked on the distance of the drop below, but I soon realized that there was a sort of handy little platform just there, with the real floor about five inches underneath. The platform had been built to hide a strange tangle of pipes of various kinds, which snaked about in the dark under the false floor. They didn't bother me, however. I soon learned which ones were hot and which weren't, and in fact, they provided several cozy little nooks and crannies, in one of which I decided to build my permanent home.

It took labor and planning, of course—what dream house doesn't? I lost count of the number of trips I made in the dead of night, carrying all kinds of lovely soft bedding material—carpet fluff, shavings, bits of chewed-up fabrics that I found carelessly left lying about (how could I know that useless-looking strip thing was Mark's school tie?). Anyway, by the time I had arranged everything to my satisfaction, a number of days had passed and I'm afraid the family had begun to despair of ever seeing me again, because I was very careful to work only after they had gone to bed in order not to draw attention to my activities.

Nobody, I was determined, was going to find this nest—it was the most beautiful I had ever constructed. Nowhere, not even in the piano, had I felt so safe and warm and comfortable. The first night I bedded down there, after feasting from a splendid supply of grain, crumbs, and (treat of treats!) raisins that I had found readily available, I felt utterly contented and pleased with myself.

There was just one thing that was not quite perfect. My under-floor home lacked a built-in water supply.

When I got thirsty I had to go out and forage for drink.

Sometimes there would be a puddle of water left on the floor near the sink, but I felt lapping up spilled water—often tasting disgustingly of detergent—was beneath my dignity.

The surest source was, of course, my own water bottle in the cage, but that meant going all the way upstairs, slithering back into the opening I had made, having a drink, and rushing home again. I could never climb in or out of the cage without making some noise, and I paid for every drink I took in this way in sheer terror that one of the boys would hear me and come out and capture me.

The infuriating thing was, there *was* water under the platform. In fact, I came to realize that one of the pipes that surrounded my nest was a water pipe. I knew this because there was a joint farther along, out of which, when the pressure was high, a few drops of water sometimes leaked. Each time this happened I would think, "How marvelous if there were a tiny hole in the pipe through which I could suck a drink whenever I wanted one!"

This thought preyed on my mind. I would often lie in bed (as you would put it), with comforting rays of light filtering through the cracks in the floorboards, and gaze at that pipe, almost willing it to spring a leak. Needless to say it didn't, but eventually, one hot night when my thirst was tormenting me and I just didn't feel like climbing mountains and running risks to get water, I decided to do something about it.

I had long ago learned that gnawing on metal is useless and painful. That was why I had not had a go at that pipe before. But what I now discovered was that not all metals are alike. I thought they were all equally hard and resistant. But as soon as I tried an experimental gnaw, I found that this kind was, well, not soft, of course not, but certainly no harder than a lot of woods.

In fact I must say that gnawing on this stuff was really very satisfying. If I didn't try to bite it, but just applied my side teeth to peeling off little threads of it, it came away beautifully. It also wore my teeth down beautifully, so that the process of actually making a hole in the thing took over a week. I didn't want to find myself with stubs instead of teeth.

I made my breakthrough on a Saturday night. I know that because the family usually lies in bed late on a Sunday, enabling me to be out and about in the morning after my usual bedtime, foraging for special tidbits for my own Sunday lunch.

On this occasion, though, there was no Sunday lunch for anybody.

At dawn, after a night's work, I sensed that I was about to pierce the water pipe. I was belly-deep in fine lead shavings. There was a long shallow channel of bright, shining metal where I was working, grooved with my toothmarks. I must be nearly there! I could feel the extra coldness of water, right against my lips as I worked. Just one more good gnaw—

Whoosh!

The next second I was flat on my back. A jet of water, which had hit me in the face and bowled me over, was making a swift-running stream across the floor. My lovely nest was awash, my

fur soaked. I jumped up and fled into a far corner out of the way of the stream, which rapidly enlarged into a river. The water as it came out of the pipe made a hissing noise every bit as sinister as the hiss of an enraged hamster. For my part, I was dumb with horror. What, oh what had I done?

I had certainly blown my hiding place and my home, that was sure. I decided that discretion, as they say, was the better part of valor. I waded across the river, which was now flowing out from under the platform over the rest of the kitchen floor, came up through my entrance hole, took one appalled look at the spreading lake, and ran as fast as my little legs would carry me to the safest place I could think of. My cage. Foolishly no doubt, I thought that if I was found there, a self-surrendered captive, suspicion would not fall on me.

I cowered in my loft, wondering what was happening downstairs and willing and willing someone to go down and stop the water before the whole house was flooded. At the same time I hoped they never would, for I could not imagine what sort of calamity would follow. Perhaps I wouldn't be blamed. I had all too little hope. The Father had become quite neurotic about me, blaming me for everything that went wrong in the house, including the loss of his hammer and the disappearance (later traced to Guy) of a two-pound box of after-dinner mints. As if I'd be caught dead eating anything so bad for my teeth! (Well, except on festive occasions!)

At last Mark got up and padded sleepily downstairs to get something to eat. I crouched with closed eyes, every nerve alert for the outcry. It came, shatteringly.

"MUMMY! DADDY! The kitchen's flooded!"

A moment later he came flying up the stairs, his face alight with excitement. I cowered down in the musty old bedding I hadn't used for weeks. The loft roof overhead was clear, and as the

Mother and Father, roused from their Sunday lie-in, came rushing down the corridor, I felt as if the ceiling were about to fall on me. What a fool I'd been to go to my cage! What a simpleton!

The whole family thundered past me and down the stairs like a herd of elephants, and I crouched, waiting for the explosion. Of course, you'll say I should have wriggled out and fled to a secure hiding place right away, but the shameful truth was I was too terrified to move. I heard the Father give voice to a bellow of dismay, while everyone else uttered shrieks and cries and exclamations and questions that went on for about ten minutes, seeming like ten hours to me. I expected every second that they would come thundering up again and rend me limb from limb. But to my great relief, nothing of the sort happened.

Slowly everything quietened down. After a bit the boys were sent upstairs to dry their feet (I assume they'd all been paddling) and get dressed. As Adam went past the cage he suddenly stopped dead.

"Look!" he cried in wonder. "It's Houdini! He's back!"

I opened one eye just long enough to see they were all crouching around me, and then I pretended to be asleep. There was such a long silence, though, that I had another peep to see why they weren't talking. The reason was, they were all looking at each other and then at me. When they did speak, it was in whispers.

"Why would he go back in by himself?"

"Unless he had a guilty conscience!"

"What's that?" hissed Guy. (It was the first time I'd heard the expression, but I knew what it meant all right!)

"He knows he did something awful, Dumbo!" Mark hissed back. "And we know what it was!"

"But we mustn't tell!" Adam said, forgetting to whisper. Mark bowled him over backward and sat on his head.

"SHHHH! If Dad ever finds out it was him—"

"If we guessed, he will too!" croaked Adam from underneath Mark.

"Then we'll take Houdini out of there and hide him somewhere else till the trouble blows over."

And that, friends, is how I found myself back in that thrice-accursed bin.

With the lid on.

chapter 7

While it was very comforting to feel that the children were on my side, it was horrible to be incarcerated in that bin, even though I had richly deserved it. I had to stay there for nearly two whole days. They fed me, of course, and let me out for a run at night after the lights were supposed to be out, but that didn't really help. To make matters worse, I lived in dread of discovery, especially after I heard Mark say, on the Monday morning:

"The plumber's coming. Daddy's taking the floorboards up."

"Daddy" was nobody's fool. I knew the minute he saw the marks of my teeth on that pipe, I was as good as done for.

The bellow he had made when he first saw the flood was but a faint whimper compared to the roar he let out when the boards came up and my crime was revealed.

"THAT ANIMAL! That—that—that little misbegotten son of a verminous flea-bitten cross-eyed sewer rat! Wait till I lay my hands on him—just wait—"

I lost my head at this point and began running around and

around inside the bin in an agony of terror. Mark heard me and lifted the lid long enough to whisper, "Keep still, you idiot! If he comes up here he'll hear you!"

Then he put the lid back and he and his brothers seemed to be dropping all sorts of stuff on top of and around the bin to hide it. I lay in the suffocating darkness and wondered whether the Father really meant even half the things he was threatening to do when he caught up with me.

Mercifully I never found out. (Incidentally I'm prepared to give him the benefit of the doubt. He's not a bad sort really; he's just got this fearful temper.) When Mark came home from school that afternoon, following a day that I would prefer to forget entirely, he had a master plan.

I was to be loaned to a neighbor, cage and all, for as long as it took the Father to calm down. I heard the boys discussing it. This neighbor also had a hamster, it seemed, so I would not be lonely. Personally I didn't care for any company whatever just then, but never mind. It would be a huge relief just to be out of the house and safe from the Father's righteous wrath.

In any case, even this disaster had not completely damped my love of change and adventure. I had pretty well exhausted the possibilities of my own family's house—I certainly had no objections to exploring another.

So, when the Father and Mother were closeted before the television, Adam popped me back into my cage and he and Mark crept downstairs, holding it between them, with Guy bringing up the rear with my bag of feed. Out of doors we went, and I had my first glimpse of the great big world of the street outside.

It was a revelation, of course. The size of it—the scope! I had had no idea, till that moment, that there was a world outside houses. Well—I suppose I had known, from pictures and TV and so on, that an Outdoors existed. But the moment I saw it, smelled it, I knew I could not rest until I had escaped from Indoors and explored the wonderful, vast, fresh-scented world of under-the-sky.

The neighbor I was to stay with proved to be a likely-looking lad, several years older than any of my boys. His hamster was a female, and the first thing they all expected of me, the moment we got inside the door, was—you guessed it. A bit of fun and games. Well. I was sorry to disappoint them, after all they'd done for me, but I really wasn't having any of that. Or so I thought till I saw her.

I won't pretend I didn't like the look of her. She was rather fetching as a matter of fact, with different colored patches on her fur—white, black, and reddish—and rather sweet little trembly whiskers. Her teeth, when she showed them to me in a not-very-friendly grimace, were really beautiful, sharp and yellow as husks of wheat. . . . But there now, I mustn't get carried away. Nothing came of it.

I don't wish to go into details, but the plain fact of the matter is, she didn't seem to find me attractive. In short, they put us together, I made a few tentative advances, just out of politeness, she bit me, and that was that. Most embarrassing. And the boys' ribald remarks didn't improve matters.

After that I was allowed to return to my cage, the top of which was firmly weighted down with several hefty books. I saw at once there'd be no getting out of that lot, so I resigned myself and went straight to bed. Fortunately this other boy knew enough to put a little cover over the clear top of my loft, which enabled me to feel very private. For all that, it took me some time to shake off a certain feeling—one most uncharacteristic of me—which I can only call humiliation. Not that I'd wanted to mate with the wretched female, you understand, especially with a lot of eager little boys urging me on in terms that I won't repeat. . . . But still. To be bitten, and with those charming little golden teeth . . . No, I won't dwell on it. No one can succeed in every field. And I consoled myself by reflecting that, if she had known what sort of hamster she was rejecting, she would have been very sorry for her rude behavior.

My own boys left, after many instructions to their pal about looking after me and especially guarding against any attempts at escape. "Don't let him out," they kept saying. "Don't let him out for a minute!" "Okay, okay," said the older boy (whose name was Ben). "Don't worry, I'm an expert." That was his opinion.

Scarcely were my boys out of the door when the cover and lid of the loft came off and I was picked up. I'd been half-asleep and was not very pleased, but I submitted myself out of courtesy to my host. First he put me in the bath, if you don't mind, and said rather jeeringly, "Let's see you escape from that, then!" Naturally I didn't give him the satisfaction of even trying—I know baths of old. I simply sat there and stared at him loftily. So then he picked me up again and carried me quite a long distance between his two cupped hands, and suddenly there was a blast of cool air and I smelled that heavenly outdoor smell again.

He put me down on an endless expanse of soft, natural-smelling green stuff—a lawn, in short. I didn't just sit staring at him now! I ran ecstatically this way and that, reveling in the feel of the grass under my feet, the scents and sounds around me that told me in no uncertain terms that here was my true element—that I was a wild creature at heart and not a tame one at all. The fact that at the end of every little run I came up against Ben's big feet planted in my way, which made me turn and run in another direction, hardly mattered. I was not—just for once—even thinking about escaping. I was simply glorying in the sensation of being more alive, more truly hamster, than I'd ever been before.

After letting me play for a while, however, Ben picked me up again. I could almost have bitten him for lifting me away from that divine grass. But in a moment my feet were sinking down into something else, something, if possible, even more exciting, more—me. It was sand.

"There you are," said Ben, in a not unfriendly tone. "That's your natural habitat if you want to know. Sorry it's not a real desert but it'll have to do."

Of course! The Mother had read aloud to the boys from a big book about how hamsters have only been discovered quite recently, in some desert country far away called the Middle East. I hadn't known till that moment what a desert was, but the minute I felt, saw, and smelled sand, I knew that a desert could be made of nothing else. How I longed to dig—to just dig and dig, burrow and burrow, till I had disappeared from view! I hadn't known till then that I had this instinct.

Now I knew, with utter certainty, that I must escape from Ben and come out into the Outdoors and find all this wonderful sand and make my home here. The great sadness I had been choking down for two days about my flooded, ruined nest under the platform just floated away. Who needed it? Here was where I belonged—Outdoors! Oh, beautiful, blissful place, where every sight and smell spoke to me of the ultimate in freedom! The largest house in the world would have seemed like a trap after that, I felt certain.

Ben was crouching beside me, watching me run hither and thither. I stopped and looked at him. He was a stranger to me. My host, yes; a friend of my boys, yes; but a stranger, and—my jailer. He had introduced me to this miracle, and for that I should be grateful; but before that he had teased me. No. I must have no scruples. I must be ruthless.

I made up my mind in that moment that I had to escape him, and that if I was forced to bite him in order to achieve my goal, then bite him I would.

chapter 8

I have made the confession that I was prepared to bite Ben because I am trying to be an honest chronicler. One must not delude oneself. Even a hamster as altogether extraordinary as myself has his weaknesses, his—I must use the word—his vices. Biting is not my vice, but escaping, if you care to look at it in that way, is. The fact that I was prepared to compromise my deepest principle in order to be free is proof of it. The equivalent, for a human being, would be wanting something so much he was prepared to hit someone over the head and steal it.

You see I don't try to minimize or excuse my fault. It was only through good luck that I was not guilty in fact, as well as in intention.

Ben let me play in the sand until it was beginning to get dark. He kept such a close watch on me that I had no chance to run. Then at last I heard a woman's voice—his Mother, presumably—calling him: "Ben! Supper time!" He turned his head to answer: "Coming in a minute!" When he turned back, I was halfway to the garden fence.

I'd already had a good look at it. It was old and as full of holes as a sock (I mean, of course, one that I've been chewing). I'd picked the particular hole I intended to make for, and the second Ben's attention was distracted I was off like a streak of lightning. This might be my last chance of freedom Outdoors, for who knew if he would ever bring me out here again? My boys had never dared—they knew me too well. So I had made up my mind that if he caught me now, I would bite him.

Fortunately—oh, how glad I am I haven't got such a thing on my conscience!—in leaping up to give chase, he tripped over the sand and fell flat. His hand, flung out after me, just touched my little bald stump of a tail as I dashed to the fence. Before he could recover, I was through and into the next garden.

You may imagine how speedily he raced out of his own back gate, and in through the gate of the garden I was now in. But it was far too late. I had summed up the geography in one glance, and shot into a big heap of sticks, leaves, and papers piled up in one corner. At once I was hidden, and with all that loose dry rustly stuff around me, you may be sure I lay still as a stone all the time he was looking for me, which he did, poor boy, until he was in a fine old state. At last his Father came, apologizing to the angry neighbor, and more or less dragged away the poor lad, who was weeping bitterly and crying, "He's not even mine and I've lost him! What'll they say to me? They'll kill me!"

To tell the truth, it was the first time I had thought of that angle. It gave me pause. Yes, indeed—my boys would be extremely upset. I didn't care to visualize the scene when they arrived at Ben's house to visit me and found me gone. For a moment I hesitated. I had only to nip back, now, through the fence, and I could make Ben the happiest boy in the world. . . . But in taking a deep breath, preparatory to doing this, I tasted again the wild, sweet air, heard again the call of natural things grow-

ing and living free—not the dead, made objects that had surrounded me all my life, but things with roots in the earth, or
things alive, with breath and blood and instincts, like me.
(Well, not really like me, of course—there was no living creature in that garden with anything like my intelligence—but
you know what I mean.)

It then became quite impossible for me to "do the decent
thing." Such a sacrifice was beyond me. I lay quietly in the heap
of garden rubbish until I heard the two back doors slam. Then I
crept out and began my first exploration of Outdoors.

At first it was quite wonderful—almost, you might say,
miraculous. I remember the Mother once reading to Guy the
story of Aladdin, a little boy whose magic lamp enabled him to
gain entrance to a cave full of treasure. The child's wonder,
amazement, and pleasure at the riches he saw heaped before
him in the cave were no greater than mine at the marvels I
found in that garden. Everything was so new to me. Not only
the strange inhabitants—worms, beetles, woodlice, etc., not to
mention birds, which nearly gave me heart failure at first . . .
but the tastes. I think I ate more that evening, just out of cu-
riosity, than ever in my life before. Grass, leaves, berries, seeds,
nuts—I even tasted a flower or two. Some were naturally more
agreeable to me than others, but it was obvious that whatever
difficulties I might get into Outdoors, I would never be hungry.

It grew dark, but of course that was nothing to me. There was
much more light here than at night in the house. I gazed up at
the sky with something close to rapture. I had heard all about
the humans' God, of course, and been quite puzzled as to what
it might be, exactly; even for an animal of my exceptional gifts,
it was hard to grasp the notion of something one couldn't see.
But now, crouched in the dark paradise of the garden, staring up
into the limitless distances above me at the bright round face

shining down kindly upon me and all my fellow creatures, I realized that this must be God. Whether it was the humans' God or not, I couldn't know; but I decided that it was definitely mine, and I sent it a Reverent Thought, which I carefully formed in my mind first:

"Let me stay under You forever."

I am very sorry to have to add that, a few minutes later, I was sending up a contrary Thought, not so much Reverent as Frantic:

"Quick! Quick! Get me back under a roof!"

chapter 9

Some huge, black, lithe shape had leapt from above and pounced on me.

I mentioned that the birds gave me a fright at first, when they flew down onto the lawn out of nowhere (as it seemed to me until I followed their flights). There was, in particular, one great big black bird which, unlike the other, smaller ones, did not fly away when I boldly ran up to it, but stood its ground with its beak agape and gave me a most evil glare. It did not actually attack me, though—it hardly occurred to me that two free creatures in the Outdoors would really wish to harm each other. Little did I know what Nature really is!

But now, without warning, I was not only attacked but in imminent danger of my life.

The villainous animal that had jumped on me with fell intent was, of course, a cat. Detestable creatures! Killers by nature—killers for sport, hunters, torturers—never, never are they to be trusted! Dogs are hunters and killers too, but they are not cruel as cats are. Excuse me if I sound prejudiced, but I have good reason. Any fears I had ever experienced in my short life till then were as nothing to the awful terror of those moments—minutes—hours?—when I was in that monster's power.

Perhaps the God above in the sky was protecting me, because otherwise, I imagine, the killer cat would have broken my poor spine with one bite. Or perhaps (here is an irony) I have the cat's wicked nature to thank for my survival. It was the brute's pleasure to keep me alive and active for a while before despatching me. Bite me it did, but not deeply enough to kill or paralyze. Just enough to make me wild with pain and fear—enough to make me run helplessly here and there while the cat jumped about, blocking my way and batting me with its paws, chiefly over the head, to keep me from thinking straight. Perhaps it had a suspicion that I was no ordinary prey, and that, if it didn't keep me half stunned with blows, I would elude it through sheer brain power.

How long this torment, physical and mental, continued, I can't say. If it had gone on much longer, I think I should have died from sheer exhaustion. But suddenly Fate took a hand.

All at once, a strong shaft of artificial light struck out into the garden, and a human figure, casting a long shadow ahead of it, strode down the path. My tormentor seemed to freeze for a second, its ugly head turned toward the figure and the light.

Had I been in my right wits, I should have been off in a flash, but as it was, I simply crouched there, trembling in every limb, my eyes starting out of my head, unable to move or even think. The figure advanced, and suddenly a man's voice said sharply, "Here! You! Be off with you!" When the cat, no doubt unwilling to abandon its prey (me), hesitated, lashing its tail, the man made a sudden sharp movement and the next moment some object clattered to the ground almost on top of the cat. It would have been on top of it, had the cat not leapt away at the last second and gone racing into the darkness. I caught a final glimpse of its hideous shape, appearing and disappearing at the top of the wall; then—thank Moon!—it was gone.

Still I didn't run. I couldn't. I was beyond moving. If the man hadn't spotted me as he came on down the garden, he might have trodden on me and that would have been the end.

However, he did see me.

"Ah, so there you are, you little villain!" he murmured. (Villain! Me! And that was without knowing that I'd been ready to bite his son!) He picked me up. "Poor little beggar—had a nasty fright, eh?" he said kindly. He put me in the big pocket of his coat.

How warm and safe I felt in there! I made no effort to get out, though there was nothing to keep me except my own weariness and fear. For the moment I had no desire at all to be free, and my devotion to the Great Outdoors had been quite knocked from my mind. Later it would return. For the moment I simply wanted to be safe.

When Ben's Father had done whatever he had to do in the garden, he went back indoors and said to his wife, "I found the hamster."

"Thank goodness for that! Poor Ben was so upset! Shall I go up and tell him?"

"No. Let him stew a bit. He shouldn't have let him out. He'll get a pleasant surprise in the morning. Now then—where's the cage?"

"In Ben's room. I wouldn't put him in there, though, you know what a racket they can make on their wheels. Pop him in with Oggi in her cage in the front room. Ben said he wants them to get together."

I stiffened. What! Spend a night with that fiend in female form? In my state of health? Never have I longed so strongly to be able to speak, to beg them to put me safely into my own cage! Didn't the fools know anything about hamsters? How they are apt to fight to the death if you put them together in one cage? Surely I had had enough for one night without being thrust into the domain of another of my own kind who had already amply demonstrated that she didn't like my company!

I began to wriggle and jump in the pocket, but a firm hand was laid on me. "Now then, now then, none of that! We'll soon have you right and tight," he said.

Horrors, horrors! I forgot the cat completely and could only think of those delectable, but razor-sharp, front teeth I had (was it possible?) so much admired at first. I must escape, I must!

Cunning. Wits and cunning must come to my aid. First I stopped struggling, and at once the guardian hand was withdrawn. I waited, motionless, until he sat down for a minute and I sensed both hands were busy (lighting a pipe as it happened). Then, using all my climbing skills, I scrambled in one quick movement out of the pocket, down his trouser leg—and away.

No time to study geography here. I just ran. Luck was with me—this was a modern kitchen, but there was a gap between the radiator and the floor. I knew those radiators can't be moved. I flung myself under it just as the man made his dive.

"Hell's bells! He's got away!" he cried. "What speed! Did you ever see anything like it?"

No, I thought, and you never will. Nothing moves as fast as I do when the devil drives! I began to recover a little confidence, thanks to his kind words of praise.

And I needed it in the next half hour. What they didn't do, the pair of them, to coax me out from under that radiator! Fortunately it wasn't on, or I'd have roasted, what with all the activity they drove me to, pushing broom handles and I don't know what else under there. But I was myself again. I would watch the thing stealthily approaching, clamber over it as it came level with me, and then wait for it to slide back the other way I had to be nimble but apart from that I really had no worries. Eventually, cursing and swearing, the man gave up. "Shut all the doors; he can't get out. I want to get to bed," he said bad-temperedly. And she must have been tired too, because in the end she left the kitchen door wide open.

So that was how I got a second complete house to explore.

It was rather different from ours. Ben's family was richer, for one thing. Rich houses aren't nearly such fun as humbler ones. Not only are appliances in the kitchen flush with each other, but the walls are smoother, the floors don't have holes in them, and there are no chimneys or ways into the space between the walls. As to drawers with broken backs, or food cupboards that won't close properly—those are right out of the question, of course.

However, there were carpets; all the soft furniture in the living room had frills right to the ground, which enabled me to do a lot of mountaineering; and there was far more space for sheer running about. I spent the first hour or so looking for a piano, but when I found it, I was disappointed; it was what they call a "grand," with nothing but thin shiny legs and no way at all to get into the works. Pity.

I didn't fancy going upstairs. Oggi the Female Fiend had her abode up there. Even if I hadn't heard them say so, I would have known, for I could smell her. It made me feel very odd, to be aware every moment that there was another hamster in the house. I won't pretend I wasn't drawn to her in a primitive sort of way, but I wasn't taking any chances.

After a night of healthy activity I became aware that dawn was coming. It now behooved me to find a secure hiding place where I could lie up for the day. This presented certain difficulties in that sort of house. There were the wastepaper baskets, of course, but they were all smooth-sided and (unlike the ones at our house, which were allowed to fill right up before anyone troubled to empty them) had hardly anything in them. I began to turn against Ben's parents. How could anyone stand living in such order, such unnatural perfection? Going around every night emptying wastepaper baskets and shutting cupboard doors—I ask you!

Anyway, I found somewhere eventually. It was a narrow, uncomfortable space behind what I learned later was a cocktail cabinet, a hideous-looking thing made of shiny pale wood. It was just about the only thing I could get behind that I thought couldn't be easily moved out. Having settled on this as a hiding place, and finding I still had a little time before the family got up, I decided to try something very difficult—to gnaw away the smooth, painted wood of the baseboard to make a bolt-hole in case I needed one.

Well! You'd think, after chewing a hole in a lead pipe, I would find this quite easy, but it wasn't. Partly, I suppose, because of the angle I had to work from—lying alongside my chewing surface and not head-on, so to speak. Besides, that paint was awful. I seemed to taste something in it that made me feel afraid. (I had felt the same about the lead, but there was no question of swallowing any of that by mistake. Little flakes of paint are different.) So after a while I had a rest from that and tried chewing the back of the cocktail cabinet instead.

This was far and away easier. In fact I'd hardly got started before I was through. Rubbish, just built for show, not like the lovely solid old furniture in our house! Even though it made life easier for me, I couldn't help despising that flimsy cabinet that let me in without even a token resistance.

The moment I broke through, I smelled food! Wasn't I ready

for it, too! With a few quick chomps around the hole, I enlarged it until I could hop through, and there, conveniently on the bottom shelf among the bottles, were three packages of mixed nuts, one of nuts and raisins, a big bag of potato chips, and a bar of milk chocolate!

What a feast! As I dug in, I couldn't help feeling rather disloyal to my newfound enthusiasm for life Outdoors, but there is no denying that, while natural, fresh-gathered seeds and green stuff are much better for you, there is a certain decadent delight about manufactured goodies. I regret to say I overindulged, especially in the chocolate, stuffing myself until I nearly burst. Then I made a rather careless nest out of the torn-up bits of wrapper and fell asleep, with fragments of chocolate still clinging to my whiskers.

chapter 10

Greed is not only disgusting. It's foolish. How many times does even a highly intelligent creature have to have this proved before the lesson sinks in?

Mind you, I don't see how I could have known that Ben's Father had a drinking problem. My boys' Father hardly touches the stuff, other than the odd beer with meals, so I naturally supposed I would have ample time to sleep off my debauch and recover my wits before the cabinet was next opened. But no. I don't think it was even lunchtime before the boozy old fellow was stealthily groping about in the interior of my hiding place for a bottle.

Overeating had put me not so much to sleep as into a stupor—evidently, or the opening of the door would have alerted me instantly. As it was, his hand was round me before I knew what was what.

I jumped. He jumped. I was the last thing he was expecting to touch and I suppose he thought I might nip him. I made a blundering dash for the hole in the back, but he was quicker.

"Got you, you little devil!"

I had never been picked up by the scruff of the neck before. Horrid indignity! Beastly discomfort! Dangling there with my back legs kicking, not able to use my teeth even if I'd been inclined to! He carried me at arm's length out of the room, up the stairs, into a room that I suppose was Ben's, and shut me securely into my cage.

Did I say securely? Well, no. Not really. Because nobody had bothered to tell him about the need for a pile of books on top of the second story, and so five minutes after he had left the room, I was out.

The scent of that female was now very strong. Maybe I would just have a look at her. After all, she couldn't get at me—she would be in a cage and I was not. I crept out of the room, following her scent, entered another room, and immediately encountered her prison.

It was on the floor straight in front of me. An ordinary cage with a wire front and metal walls. She lay asleep in a corner of it, half covered with wood shavings. Her multicolored side rose and fell delicately as she slept. I could see one little soft, round ear just twitching alluringly.

How sweet she looked lying there! How touchingly innocent, how adorable, how unaggressive! I crouched by the wire mesh, gazing and gazing at her. I forgot her savage attack on me, or rather, I couldn't believe in it. I just longed and longed to be in there with her, her established and acknowledged mate.

I had heard a great deal about Love while living with my family. I had grown up in the knowledge that they loved each other, despite all the shouting and quarreling that went on. I came more or less to understand that it was a deep feeling of wanting to be with someone, of knowing that somehow you belonged to each other. It was something I never expected to feel myself—I

thought that hamsters, being naturally solitary and freedom-seeking, would be incapable of such an attachment, which must bind you to a fellow creature as surely as you are bound to a miserable, limited, dependent existence inside a cage.

But now, looking at Oggi, I knew something of Love. I knew the desire to get close, instead of my usual desire, which was to get away.

I stayed there for hours, mesmerized by her beauty.

Suddenly she opened her little black beady eyes.

The moment she saw and smelled me, she leapt to her feet in one jerky movement and crouched there, facing me. All illusion of innocence and mildness vanished. She lifted her lip and showed her teeth to me—she even chattered them a bit, just in case I hadn't got the message. I backed off a little before I could control myself (the bite she'd given me still smarted), but then, remembering she couldn't get out, I crept boldly back, my eyes fixed on her. I was not going to let any cheeky little patch-coated she-hamster see she had me scared.

Hamsters cannot communicate with each other by voice, but they can send signals. I now sent a very simple, primitive signal that I knew she would understand even if she was stupid:

I want to mate with you.

Swift as thought, she sent me one back!

Nothing doing. Be off.

Well, this was a blow, but I was not to be daunted this time by any fear of humiliation. I was determined. So I sent:

You're very beautiful and I'm going to mate with you whether you like it or not.

(This would doubtless seem high-handed to a human being, but a buck has to be firm with his doe. Does don't appreciate halfheartedness; you have to show them who's boss.)

Her reply was:

You can't anyway. There's no way into my cage.

But I noticed she wasn't chattering her teeth anymore.

I sent: *Leave that to me.* I sent this with a (I admit) rather cocky little flick of my whiskers. How I would get in, I hadn't a clue, but she didn't know that. She just saw that I had confidence, that nothing was going to stand between us, not even metal walls and wire mesh. To my joy I saw her relax, just a fraction. Her lip came down, covering those teeth, and—no, I wasn't mistaken—a softer look appeared in those little shiny black eyes. She even moved fractionally nearer to me.

If she had been at all clever, she might have sent a question now, as to how I meant to get to her, but she wasn't clever and I didn't want her to be. I didn't want an intellectual challenge; I wasn't looking for a partner in life, or a like minded companion. I wanted a mate. This one and no other. And I meant to have her.

I stepped boldly to the mesh and sent, *Come close. Smell me. You'll like me when you get used to my smell.*

Now she had lost her aggression, she was shy. She wouldn't come at first. But I sent soothing, inviting signals and at last she edged closer and closer until our noses were touching through a mesh hole. Not actually touching—just quivering, so close that the hairs vibrated together. Delicious ecstasy! Better than chocolate, better than the air Outdoors, better than staring up in reverence at my round, white God in the sky. How grateful I was to have learned about Love so that I could understand my situation and my feelings!

Suddenly she sent, *Come on then, what are you waiting for?*

Good Moon, what was I to do now? How could I make good my recent boast? I backed off slightly and gave her cage a quick once-over. Not a hope. Everything, as the man said, right and tight—not a bit of torn wire or a loose corner to be seen. Nothing for it but a bit of bluff, so I sent:

Patience, doe! All in good time.

Looking rebuffed, she retreated to her sleeping corner and turned her back on me. Can't blame the poor little thing really. I felt like such a fool. I must make a plan.

Two opposite impulses now tugged at me. The first, my usual one, was to make myself scarce; my time sense, which I had been developing lately, told me that it was nearly time for Ben to come home from school. The opposite impulse said, No. Stay here, near Oggi's cage. Ben will find you and realize the situation. He wants Oggi bred. He'll put you in with her, and then— happy days!

So that's what I did. I just crouched by the cage, and after a short time I heard Ben coming up the stairs. Oh, how I had to fight down all my usual escape instincts! But Oggi was staring at me again, waiting to see what I would do, and so I managed just to sit tight.

In he came, looking gloomy, but not for long. His face positively lit up when he saw me, and with a whoop that would have sent me shooting off if I had not made my decision, he pounced on me.

"Houdini! Houdini!" he cried, and did a clumsy sort of dance round the room, holding me in front of him, jouncing and bouncing till I felt quite queasy. I did wish he wouldn't, in front of my female too—it was too undignified for words. But at last he stopped dancing and brought me close to his face. His boy breath was not as congenial to me as Mark's, but I put up with it.

"What are you doing in here, you little devil?" he asked. "Want another go at her, do you? Okay then."

Really, how boys express themselves these days! Too gross.

He opened the wire and put me inside the cage.

"Watch it, now, Houdikins," he said roguishly. (Houdikins indeed!) "Don't let her see you off so easy this time!"

She didn't "see me off," but neither was she very forthcoming, and I was glad of that. No public performances for me, thank you! We just sat at opposite sides of the cage looking at each other and I sent signals about waiting till we were alone, which she evidently agreed with, bless her modest little heart. At long last Ben got fed up.

"Just remember what the hamster book says," he grumbled to me. "After you've done it, keep clear of her. She's as bad as a black widow spider—she'll have your guts for garters if you don't look out."

With that he took off, calling ahead of him, "Mom! Could you come up and keep an eye on the hamsters while I run over and get Mark? I think they're going to mate!"

But his Mother must have been busy just then, or maybe she had some decent instincts, because she left us alone for—well, to be honest I rather lost track of the time, what with one thing and another. But it was long enough.

chapter 11

Well! A human male, I believe, would now call himself well wedded and bedded, but it's different for us hamsters. The moment our union was complete (and though I have no wish to be indelicate, I must say that the experience was by no means a disappointment to either of us), a total change of mood came over Oggi and me. We began to fight. Oh, not savagely, just rather playfully, but we were each making it clear to the other that we were independent creatures who, for the moment at any rate, had no wish to waste more solitary time being together.

Her nips and scratches were not humiliating to me now. I would have hated it if she had got possessive and started clinging around me. She was "seeing me off," as Ben put it, in the way of our kind, and nothing could have suited me better or made me respect her more. Dim in mind she might be, poor thing, but all her hamster instincts were functioning properly. In a word, she pleased me, and though all thoughts of Love had vanished, I was well satisfied with the whole episode.

Our little battle had no time to get out of hand, for Ben's

Mother soon arrived, suitably gloved, and separated us. I was put back in my cage, where, feeling excessively tired (it was, after all, the middle of the day, not normally my active time), I was quite glad to retire to my loft and drop off to sleep, after giving myself a good grooming.

I must have been even more tired than I realized. I was aware of some swaying and other movements, but I was quite astonished, on waking, to find myself back in my former home. Peering out of my loft, I saw that my escape route had been cut off—the boys, evidently informed of my escapades at Ben's, were taking no chances and had heaped so many books on the top of my cage that ten hamsters couldn't have shifted them.

I spent uncountable days imprisoned. The boys fed me and kept my water bottle refilled but I was not let out at all. I did my best to persuade them, by standing on my hind legs every time they came near and reaching my forepaws through the ventilation bars, or pushing my nose through in what I hoped was a beseeching fashion, but they were not to be moved. The Father must have made his views very clear on the subject of what would befall the next boy who allowed me to escape.

I was not idle. One must never be idle, even in prison—perhaps especially not there, when one can so easily fall into depression and allow mind and body to stagnate. I found plenty to do.

Instead of moping, I followed this sensible routine: On waking from my day's sleep I would groom myself, have a light snack, and give myself some healthy exercise on my wheel. Then I would shift my bedding around to air it, sometimes moving it down from the loft to another part of the cage for a change. I would sort over my store of feed, placing special tidbits like nuts or sunflower seeds aside so that I could treat myself occasionally.

Then I would settle down to learn.

I did this primarily by listening to, and observing, the humans around me. Their behavior and conversation taught me a great deal.

I also watched television. The boys had a little black-and-white set of their own in the room (Guy's) where I most often was, and I liked to sit and gaze at it in the evenings. Regrettably, the boys' tastes are not as elevated as mine. I would have relished more documentaries, especially animal ones, but alas! These often clashed with things called rock shows, a deplorably lowbrow form of entertainment, which frankly bored me stiff, but the boys reveled in them and would never switch over to the more intellectual offerings until the last song had been squawked and the last drum beaten to death.

The remainder of my time, in the dead of night, was spent as you would expect—in trying to devise escape plans.

I thought if I could shift that roof the least fraction, the heavy books might slide off, and I tried it, but after nearly straining my back, I had to give up. I worked long and hard on the plug to the entrance hole, but it was no use—I just couldn't budge it.

So then I had to content myself by thinking and dreaming of what I would get up to when at last they relented and let me out. I never let myself doubt that it would happen. Nobody could be so cruel as to keep me caged up forever, for they knew my nature now—they knew what I craved. What they did not know was that I now craved freedom Outdoors as well as in.

No, I had not forgotten my hair-raising adventure with the cat. (It was, incidentally, only during this period, while watching a children's program, that I discovered the name of my persecutor, and that, far from hating the breed, most children love them. It appalled me to see those nice, unsuspecting people on the screen actually petting and caressing the brutes as if they were as worthy of human devotion as—well, as I am myself!

Shocking misplacement of affection! Unmerited reward for an evil, deceitful nature!)

No, I had not forgotten. But now I knew of the danger, I felt convinced I could be on my guard against it. A hamster who lives Outdoors, I realized, must have eyes on the top of his head. While in my cage, I practiced glancing quickly upward without cricking my neck, as well as performing swift little turns and leaps in all directions. I finally managed a complete half-turn in one jump. The one thing I couldn't practice, and this worried me, was long-distance sprinting. I knew I would get out sometime. I wanted to be ready.

In the end my patience and faith were rewarded.

One day, during school hours, the Mother came to clean up Guy's room, which desperately needed it I may say—terribly untidy child, Guy. I was asleep at the time, but the vacuum cleaner woke me, and I at once went into my well-known "let me get out for pity's sake" routine. Usually she studiously ignored me when I was doing this, but now she crouched down beside my cage and, putting out her finger, rubbed the tip of my nose as I pushed it through the bars.

"Poor old Houdini," she murmured. "It's been a long time, hasn't it? What about a little run in the bathroom? You can't get out of there, and it'll give your poor legs a stretch."

I positively went mad when she said that, reaching both front paws through the bars and uttering subsonic squeaks. She seemed startled and said, "You funny little beast! One would swear you understood every word!"

With this ignorant and unflattering observation, she unplugged the opening and I shot out into her hands.

Palpitating with joy, I was carried into the bathroom. In earlier, happier days the boys would often take me in there to play while they had their baths, so I knew the small room well—far better, in fact, than the Mother, which was one reason I was so excited I could hardly contain myself.

I hoped she would put me straight onto the floor and then leave me alone, in which case I could have put my master plan into operation immediately. She was not taking any chances, however. She did indeed put me on the floor, after carefully closing the door, but she stayed there with me for quite a while, cleaning various bits of the room; while that was going on, I simply ran about in apparently innocent enjoyment and didn't even go near the door, to avoid arousing her suspicions.

However, when she had finished, she picked me up. My heart sank. Was it to be back to the cage?

But no—my luck was in.

"You can play in the bath for a bit," she said, "if that's any fun for you."

Well, of course, it would have been deadly, but for one miraculous thing. She left the rubber shower attachment hanging off the faucet into the bathtub, little dreaming, I suppose, that I would be up it like greased lightning the second she was out of the room.

Now, I mentioned that this was an old house, and a rather shabby one. The Father, fortunately for me, was no do-it-yourself expert; otherwise that space between the rounded corner of the bath next to the wall, and the wall itself, would long ago have been filled in. As it was, it was the work of a moment to jump down this opening onto the boarded floor, and from there make my way to the hole leading to the Outdoors, which I had known about ages ago from the draft of fresh air that always came to me in that room.

The hole was a small one, through which, I imagine, some waste pipe or other had once been fitted, but it was gone. I poked my head through the brickwork and looked down. Down!

I tell you, that's not the word! I've done a bit of vertical jumping in my life but this was ridiculous. I could hardly see the ground (my eyes are no use for distances). Every instinct I had warned me away from that brink— a jump, or fall, from such a height would kill me.

But I had to get down, nonetheless. How to do it?

I forced myself to overcome my fear and look again. This time, off a little to one side, I noticed something that at once terrified me and filled me with elation.

It was a drainpipe, which ran down the whole side of the house. The top of it, not more than twice my length from the hole I sat in, was shaped like a funnel. I had only to pluck up my courage for a powerful sideways leap, and then a bit more for a long, vertical dive down that pipe, and I would be free.

I did not hesitate any longer than it took me to gather my haunches under me and shift my weight once or twice to get ready. Then I fairly launched myself across the yawning gap.

Because I had not had a proper launching platform, but had had to jump out of the hole, I nearly missed. The horror of it comes back to me now in waves of fear. That drop! The hard pavement below! But the worst did not happen. True, I didn't land in the funnel. But the front half of me did, enough to enable me to clutch the rough rim of the funnel with my forepaws and lean my head and shoulders over it for balance, so by kicking and scrabbling with my strong back legs and claws, I was able to heave myself in.

My heart was thudding so hard in my chest that, if I'd had a choice, I would have paused in the mouth of the pipe to give myself a chance to recover. However, no such choice was mine. I had tipped myself so violently over the edge that I couldn't stop and just went hurtling headfirst down the pipe.

It was much like my tubes in the cage, but a bit wider, so that it was much harder for me to brake with my back and feet against the sides. I felt myself literally falling and had to make a sort of half-somersault inside the pipe to slow myself down. This jarred me, which hurt quite a bit, but at least it broke my fall, and after that I was able to control my descent better. After a few seconds, I saw light rushing to meet me, and next moment I was out.

chapter 12

Free! Free! Free!

I have already mentioned that I am not conceited, but if ever there was a moment for justifiable pride, it was surely now. By my own unaided efforts, by my wit, my skill, my courage, I had freed myself. Who among hamsters could have avoided a feeling of self-satisfaction? Indeed, if I could have danced, I would have, right there on the smelly grating at the bottom of the drainpipe.

As it was, I lost no time in hopping out and running down the paved passage alongside the house and into the back garden.

It was midday. Feeling a sudden warmth on my back as I emerged from the shadows of the house, I quickly looked up— then had to close my eyes. I knew it was the sun shining down upon me, but I had not known it would feel so wonderful, like a blessing laid on my fur, nor that I would be quite unable to look this new marvel in the face. Instantly I abandoned my old, cold, pallid God of the night and adopted this evidently much more powerful new one.

I should add that I am not, even now, truly converted to religion. It's nice to have some Big Thing in one's life to send the occasional Reverent Thought or Signal to in time of trouble, but frankly I don't feel the need very often. I'm too self-reliant. But I did think it worthwhile on this occasion to send a Hope, that cats do not hunt by day.

I don't mean, of course, that having sent a Hope to my new God, I relaxed my vigilance—that would never do. I kept a watchful eye all about me as I advanced down the garden; but apart from birdsong above and the minute whispering of little crawling things in the earth below, all was perfectly quiet and peaceful.

I moved slowly, exploring as I went. The scents and even tastes had subtly changed since I had been Outdoors at Ben's. There were leaves scattered on the ground now, covering the grass—leaves too dry to be good to eat. But there were many more seeds and berries—I found a whole bush of the sort that had tempted me onto the mantelpiece so long ago, and ate my fill of them again.

There was something in the air, too, that had not been there before—a mysterious tang, a little like the beginnings of fear, yet somehow not unpleasant but more like the first surge of some great pleasure. I felt, when I had eaten and run about, a new sensation, of mellowness and laziness and warmth. Was it just that I was not used to being up and about by day? Was it simple sleepiness? Perhaps, I thought, as I curled up in a pleasant little nest burrowed in a pile of dry leaves, perhaps it was just that pride I spoke of before. But it surely went deeper than that.

I drifted into one of the most pleasant dozes of my life. I was too excited, too aware of possible dangers, to sleep soundly, but I did drift off, and I had some strange experiences in my half-sleep, which must be like what humans call visions. I seemed to be carried up into the very mouth of the Sun God himself. There I was, far from my own world, a part of another.

And the Sun God sent me a signal: *Make your nest in a safe place and lay by a store. You must die a little death. But you will not die forever. Only while I am weak and chilly. When I recover my strength, you will get your life back, so fear nothing.*

And I signaled back: *I am not afraid.*

With that the Sun God swallowed me up and I became part of him. And it was beautiful.

Beautiful—but hot.

I woke with a start. I was half suffocated with a thick, choking cloud that swirled round me. My ears were full of an awful crackling noise. And worst of all, I found myself hemmed in by heat—terrible, glowing heat that singed my fur.

I jumped about in frenzied jerks, facing all directions in a split second. All around me was something new, something I instinctively recognized as the worst thing in the world. Fire.

For a few terrible seconds, fear paralyzed me. I watched the red horror creeping around me, forming red bars of the most awful cage of my life. The most awful, and the last—unless I could pass through it and save myself.

An ordinary hamster would have crouched there, numb and helpless with fear, until he perished. I was different.

I forced myself to look all around me once more. There was one place and one only where the flames had not yet taken a strong hold on the leaves. One long leaf, its dry edges just fringed with fire and curling upward like a live thing in the smoke, lay before me—a low place in the wall of fire. I couldn't see what lay beyond it, but I had to take the chance that, in jumping over it, I would land in the heart of the inferno.

I am not a gerbil—a high jump from a standstill is not part of my natural armory. Still, I had to try. Once more I gathered my hindquarters under me. No, it was impossible! The flames were rising. I must take a run at it! I edged backward.

Something seemed to catch hold of my little bare tail and give it an agonizing bite. I had thrust it right into a hot ember. Instantly I bounded forward. Blinded by smoke and terror, I felt myself kicking in midair as if to drive myself on, yet I was sure I was jumping to a painful death.

But no! When I opened my eyes, I was lying on the grass. My whiskers were singed, my tail blistered—but what was that, compared to what could have happened? I crawled further from the heat, trying to control my trembling, then dared to look back. I was still half in my dream, half in a daze of mingled panic and relief. Was it the sun itself that had come to earth to consume me?

Behind me was my heap of leaves, into which I had crawled earlier to make my safe napping nest. The harmless pile was now a hellish hill of smoke and flame. Standing beyond it, tending it and feeding it with more leaves, was the boys' Father. It must have been he who had turned my happy resting place into a dangerous inferno and nearly roasted me alive!

For one ignoble moment I hated him. I thought he had done it on purpose. Then charity and good sense reasserted themselves. Of course not! How could he know I was in there? I had no business to be. The fault, if there was a fault, was mine. I'm glad to say I forgave him instantly for the terrible fright I had had, and for my poor sore tail.

You may well suppose that, what with cats and bonfires, I might now be quite disillusioned with Outdoors and long for nothing but to crawl back up that drainpipe again. No such thing. My adventures, I decided, were just beginning. I ran to a flower bed and hid in a clump of living leaves. Their coolness was blissful; they closed over me like a gentle wave. Speaking of waves, I was desperately thirsty; but by smelling around I soon found enough water on the leaves around me, though it was not as easy or satisfying as sucking on my bottle.

Never mind, I thought, I must not be fussy! Never let it be said that Houdini had become soft, spoiled, or decadent through a life of dependence and luxury Indoors. I had passed many tests—tests of skill, cleverness, and bravery. Now it was up to me to show that I could pass tests of endurance and adaptability.

The first came soon enough. I had been through my ordeal by fire. Next came one by water.

At evening I woke among the leaves, ready, as I thought, for anything. I felt shivery—a reaction to my narrow escape perhaps. But no. The sun had disappeared behind a heavy lid of blackness that was not the blackness of night, with its brilliant points of light and its gleam of infinite distances, but a dreary, threatening blackness that seemed to hang close overhead. Even as I looked up at it, missing the awesome kindly face of my new God, big drops of water began to splash down upon me.

As I had not guessed from pictures of the sun that it was hot and comforting, I had not guessed of rain that it was wet and would make me so utterly miserable. In a few minutes I was soaked to the skin and must have looked half my normal size, as all my fur was plastered to me. I scurried hither and thither, looking for shelter. There was none—not even a tree, and the bushes, all but leafless, gave little protection from the downpour, which grew heavier and heavier until I was looking and feeling like a drowned rat. The only good thing was that the cold water took some of the sting out of my burned tail.

After huddling wretchedly against a leaning fence for as long as I could bear, hoping the rain would stop, I summoned up my spirits. "You wanted to live free Outdoors," I admonished myself. "This is part of it. Come along now! No weakening—" (You see, I had caught myself thinking longingly of my warm dry loft, lined with flannel.) "Be yourself! Take command of the situation! This garden isn't the whole of Outdoors, you know!"

Purposeful activity is, of course, the best antidote to cold and discomfort. I made a dash for the back gate, squirmed under it (muddying my belly), and found myself in a dismal alley between high walls. However, right away I was rewarded, for there was a garbage can lid, left off no doubt by one of those careless garbagemen the Mother was forever grumbling about, lying propped against the wall at an angle. In a flash I was under it. I won't say it was warm or comfortable under there, nor that the smell was exactly enticing, but at least it was dry. For the first time I understood what my boys had meant when they spoke of the pleasures of lying in bed listening to the rain beating on the roof, feeling glad to be out of it and sorry for anyone who wasn't.

chapter 13

If I had but known the danger I stood in every minute I was Outdoors, I would not have blamed myself for weakness because I wanted, many times, to scuttle Indoors again. I would have thought myself simply prudent and sensible. No normal hamster, raised as a pet, could have survived for an hour. How I passed nearly two nights and days in the open, and lived to tell the tale, I shall never know. Obviously cleverness accounted for a lot of my escapes; yet in honesty I must say that I owe my survival mainly to luck.

Outdoors is *perilous*. As for Nature —! No words, even of mine, could describe the horrors I witnessed to someone who had only seen the great world of the Open Air through a window or on a television screen. The violence! The ruthlessness! A continuous nightmare, I assure you.

Danger, for some creature or other, was everywhere. Even as I sheltered beneath the garbage can lid, I observed the sickening sight of a big brown bird bashing a snail to death against a wall and eating it. Of course such sights became so commonplace before long that I scarcely turned a hair at them, but that first incident made a dreadful impression. Then, just as the rain was stopping, and I was peeping out to see if all was safe, I was appalled to see a great black shaggy animal ambling along the alley, nose down, sniffing out its prey.

The brown snail-basher flew off, but what could I do? The thing was vast—ten times the size of a cat. I looked with horror at its great jaws, which could very easily have snapped me in two with one bite. Nearer and nearer it came. Should I run? My instincts of self-preservation were dulled through long disuse. One said, "Yes, run! It's slow-moving, it won't catch up if you go now!" Another said, "Keep still and it may not notice you!" These two conflicting impulses warred within me for several seconds as the shaggy brute drew nearer. Finally it seemed too late to heed the first, so I obeyed the second.

That's what I mean by luck. I soon realized the silly great thing was not interested in me but only in the contents of the open garbage can. If I had run, however, it would doubtless have given chase just for the fun of it and might have killed me for the fun of it too—I really don't think it had the wit to kill me for any sensible reason such as to get food. . . . Anyway it was simply bulging with fat.

It put its clumsy forefeet up onto the rim of the garbage can, and immediately, of course, the can fell over, scattering its contents all over the alley. That was the last I saw of the creature, or anything else, for some time.

Had I not so recently feared for my life at the teeth of that scavenging animal, I would have been terrified. For there was a crash, and the next second, all was dark—a total darkness I had never experienced before—and I knew I was in a new kind of prison. The fall of the garbage can had knocked my leaning lid flat, on top of me.

This time I kept my head. Well, I thought, sitting down in the middle where the headroom was greatest, at least nothing can get to me while I'm under here. Still, as time went by I began to get alarmed. I tried to push the thing, but it was too heavy. I tried to raise it with my back—no luck. Then I tried digging under it, but the alley was not sand—it was some kind of hard-packed grit. I could do it, I felt, eventually, but it would be an exhausting struggle. Still, there was no other way out, so I set to work.

I had never dug in my life. My paws hardly knew the way. And believe me, this was no surface to begin on! Before I'd been at it long, my forepaws were so sore I could hardly go on, and my back legs were aching from being braced against the ground and kicking back the stuff I dug up.

I could soon see and smell that I had made a little gap, but how I was going to make it big enough to crawl through I didn't know. My front paws felt terrible, as if they might be going to bleed. I had to stop and give them a rest. And that was when my next bit of luck occurred.

I heard footsteps, then the creak of the gate. I poised myself for instant flight, for I recognized the Mother's steps and I guessed what would happen. It did. She stopped, made that tut-tutting noise by which humans, especially females, express annoyance, and the next moment the lid was lifted.

It was now almost night (my luck again!). She saw me, all right, but she was so taken by surprise that long before she could grab me (she had her wastebasket in her other hand), I was off.

The poor woman actually called me as if I'd been a dog myself.

"Houdini! Houdini! Come back!" she cried forlornly as I fled down the alley. A pang of conscience smote me, but not very hard. I kept going. At least none of the boys would get into trouble for freeing me. From my observations of human family life, it does no harm, every now and then, for a parent to do the silly thing and give the poor young ones a chance to do the blaming and scolding. Anyway I can never get very concerned about humans when my freedom is at stake.

I knew she was after me, so I speedily ducked under another garden gate, and long before she panted up, I had concealed myself under a pile of bricks. I was prepared for a long, exciting hunt through the darkness, but rather to my disappointment, she gave up almost at once.

I waited till her footsteps died away. Then I took careful stock of my situation.

The garden I was in now was a large one. It contained trees, plants and bushes galore, a large lake (well, I suppose it would be a small pond to a human), a pile of rocks with things growing between them—full of wonderful hiding places—and, best of all to me, a big area of sand, which, I was surprised and puzzled to discover, was already full of little hillocks and tunnels, all well made and smoothly finished, as if specially for me.

I explored all night, always keeping my ears and nose open for warnings of the approach of danger. Twice I smelled the hated smell of a prowling cat. Once I dashed back under the bricks, and the other time I dived into one of the ready-made sand tunnels. I didn't know whether cats could dig. I suspected they could, and when this one slouched nearer, I faced up the tunnel toward it, preparing to fight for my life. But it seemed the cat had some other business in the sandy area—personal business—and when this was completed to its satisfaction (I must admit cats have very dainty habits in some things), it slid off into the darkness again without troubling me any further.

I practiced digging in the sand—a far cry from the harsh labor in the alley—but my paws were too sore to do much even here, and besides, I was growing sleepy. This was odd—it was not morning yet. Most unlike me to lose energy before daylight came. Perhaps it was the fresh air and all my adventures. At all events this wouldn't do. I must look for a really safe place to sleep.

I found it in the rock pile, a little cave, its mouth masked with trailing leaves from above. It was dry inside, and I found some dead leaves that were not too crackly and rough, and dragged them in for bedding. The last few I brought seemed extraordinarily heavy. Really it was most odd how tired I felt.

After just nibbling some wet grass for a nightcap, I entered my first Outdoor home. How free and independent I felt! How sweet was the crisp night air, how pleasant the satisfaction of having survived so many hazards! Even my sore paws and tail were no longer simply painful. I gained a sort of pleasure from aches I had got in the course of learning to be a wild animal.

chapter 14

It was quite late the following night before I woke up again.

Funny, I thought, I went to sleep early, and here I am, waking up long after my usual time. Am I getting old, or what?

One thing I have never succeeded in working out was how long hamsters live—perhaps because I preferred not to know. The words "two years," read out of the *Enjoy Your Hamster* book, meant nothing to me. For all my brilliance I had never learned how to measure time, beyond days and nights. How many of these might constitute a year I didn't know. But I did know that all creatures age and die, though till a few hours ago I had never seen a dead creature. Perhaps that was why the death of that snail upset me so much.

Now I lay, still curiously drowsy, in my cave, looking out at the night through the gently stirring leaves that hid me from prowling predators, and wondered if old age was creeping up on me. I hoped not. I was not ready to get old. On the contrary! I remembered the amazing details of my escape from the house and

I knew I was in my prime. Yet why this sudden need for extra sleep?

Well, it was a mystery I couldn't solve, so I didn't waste time on it. I shook myself briskly awake. At least I wasn't losing my appetite! I was famished. I poked my nose cautiously through the screen of leaves and sniffed the night air. It was innocent of any hint of peril. I came out, and after double-checking that all was well, I began my nightly forage.

I was just polishing off some extremely tasty berries when I became aware of a small animal quite close to me. Instinct reassured me—there was nothing to fear. Nevertheless I froze and watched it approach through the gloom.

It was not unlike a much smaller version of myself, except that its nose was more pointed and it had a long thin tail. Also it was of a nondescript gray, rather than my beautiful gold. But it was clearly somewhat kin to my species, and as it came up to me, I realized it was a field mouse.

It seemed to be in some distress. I sent it a hamster signal. It's hard to put such signals into human language because, as between animal and animal, words do not really play any part. My signal was a mixture of greeting and inquiry, a Hello-are-you-all-right? sort of message. There was no coherent answer, just a lot of trembling of whiskers and desperate looks. It was afraid of me, evidently, so I wondered why it came so close. Perhaps there was something else it feared even more?

I looked all around again carefully. Nothing—at least nothing I could see, hear, or smell. But the mouse sensed something. Suddenly it sent me a clear signal that any fool could have understood: "Danger! Run!" At almost the same instant it took off, rushing wildly away in a zigzag dash across the lawn.

I watched it go, puzzled, uneasy, and yet feeling rather superior, for who with any sense would run into the open like that? Better to crouch in the shadows of the bush until the danger had passed. As I watched, the mouse stopped dead, seeming to shrink into itself, and I lost sight of it for a moment because it was so still in the dark. And then, out of nowhere, out of the very sky, a great winged shape swooped down.

I lay rooted to the ground, every muscle taut with horror. I saw the broad wings, the spread pinions, the round head—and the outstretched talons. I heard the thin shriek, cut off fur-raisingly in the middle. The predator did not alight. All in one movement it beat up again from the shadowy ground, and a moment later I could see it, outlined against the stars as it soared away on silent motionless wings. I could not see the poor little dead thing it carried, but I knew it was there.

I did not move for a long, long time. It was not just fear. It was shock. A snail—well, that was one thing. A lower form of life, and after all, we must all eat. But a warm-blooded, furry creature, capable of fear, of pain—to be snatched from life like that before my very eyes—it was just too horrible. It was some time before I could take it in.

But when I had, I knew for certain that Outdoors was not just another name for freedom. It was a name for Nature, and Nature was a name for sudden death. Death here was not a mere occasional accident, caused by rare and perverse villains; it was part of a pattern, in which any form of life might find itself destroyed before its time, to make sport or food for some other form. Neither sun nor moon nor any other power could prevent it. Speed and caution, wit and cunning might help one stay alive—but in the end, superior strength must prevail. Lying there on the sweet, natural earth, my belly full of the unbloody food of my innocent appetite, I knew the truth: If I stayed out here in the open, if I indulged my longing for freedom, sooner or later I would lose my life. Cat, or dog, or great winged bird— one of them, or some other killer that I had still to meet, would outwit or outfight me some dark night or warm drowsy midday. That is, if I were not set light to, or stepped on, or trapped, or drowned, or in some other way disposed of.

Now I must face the ultimate question. All my life I had lived for freedom. Now I had it. Did I, when the crunch came, want it at this cost?

I forced my stiff legs to move at last, and in one panic-stricken dash I regained my cave in the rocks. With fast-beating heart I lay there, asking the question again and again. Freedom—and death? Or captivity—and safety?

It may seem that I have shown some small degree of satisfaction with myself and my doings throughout this history. If that has been the case, I apologize, for nothing is more offensive to me than any kind of bombast or undue conceit. I say undue because, of course, there is a just conceit, a pride that is deserved, and to deny that is mere imitation modesty, a lie, in fact. For it can't be denied, even by me, that many of my exploits showed exceptional qualities.

But now comes the moment in my life of which I am proudest, and even if I had had an even more astonishing tale to tell of myself until this point, I would say that all my bravery, skill, and intelligence till now counted for very little beside the true heroism of my answer to this vital and terrible question.

I decided to stay Outdoors, and if I had to die for it, well! A short life and a merry one, as humans say. And if not so very merry (as seemed likely after the grim events of the night), then at least—free.

I celebrated this magnificent decision by emerging boldly from my cave, running to the base of the rock pile, and scampering round it once or twice as if tempting all the terrors of the night to do their worst. So full of courage was I that I swear I half hoped some cat or bird of prey would attack me, for I felt sure I could do justice to myself. I felt a hero and I longed to prove it! And all of a sudden, the chance came.

And I muffed it.

Oh, the shame of it! The awful anticlimax! I can scarcely bear to relate what happened, and would gladly skip over it if I were not so honest.

But was it not an irony of fate that that grand climax of my life should have been all but spoiled by the wretched, humiliating accident that immediately followed?

It was not even some really ferocious foe that was my undoing. It was a dog. The selfsame fat, lumbering, shaggy beast who had nosed his way up the alley and upset the garbage can. How I came to be caught by such an idiotic slow-moving lump I do not know, and never will. No doubt I was so carried away with my noble decision that my nose and other senses temporarily ceased to function.

For the creature must have been nearby for some minutes and have seen me come out of the cave and run about with foolish bravado. The second time I rounded the corner of the rock pile, I ran straight into its mouth.

I made one ludicrous attempt to bite or jump free, but it was hopeless. He closed his jaws on me—I smelled his crude breath and felt the tightening of his huge teeth—I knew it was all over with me, and my last thought (as I supposed) was: At least I will die silently.

But I did not die! The teeth closed, but only until I was held fast between them. They did not so much as bruise my back. I felt myself being carried quite gently and, opening my eyes, saw that we were approaching the back door of a house. The dog raised a heavy forepaw and scratched. After a few moments it opened and the dog stepped in.

I was Indoors.

chapter 15

Little did I know, as I was carried through that back door-way, that the worst ordeal of my life was about to begin.

I have so far described two human homes—the one I call ours, a rather old-fashioned and modest one; and Ben's, which was very modern and smart, if you care for that sort of thing.

The house I now entered, all unwillingly, was very different from either. When that dimwitted (but, I must say, gentle) dog deposited me on the kitchen floor, I had a quick look round—and wondered, for a moment, if I was in a home at all, or if this was some sort of roofed extension of Outdoors. But the smell alone soon put the notion from my mind. Outdoors has a smell that I love, and that is principally—from my height—of earth. To some humans, Mothers especially, earth is just another word for dirt, especially when it is on their children's bodies. But let me assure them that no two substances could be more different to one with a sensitive nose like mine.

This house simply stank of dirt. It was awful. There was stale food in it, and unwashed human bodies, and dog, of course—a great deal of dog. But there was another smell, one I recognized from that cupboard I was in at Ben's, the one with all the bottles. Later I learned it was called Alcohol.

And everywhere was rubbish.

It was not just the sort of untidiness and mess I was used to at our house. That got cleared up reasonably often (the Father called it a blitz) and the surfaces under it swept and washed. Soon they were covered with clutter all over again, but that deep stench of piled-up filth certainly never happened there. All my senses fairly reeled back from it when it hit me.

The whole room was littered with dirty, broken, ugly, uninviting junk. I say "uninviting" because usually, as soon as I see objects scattered about, I want to run under and over them and explore them; but no fastidious animal in his right mind would have wanted to go anywhere near this lot. It looked as if some giant creature had run amok there, knocking things over, breaking them, spilling things all over them—and then leaving them, for a long, long time, to get covered with dust and grease.

Could the dog have done this? At the thought my blood ran cold, for only an animal completely mad could have caused such havoc, and madness is the most fearful thing in an animal, something we all avoid even thinking about.

But I reassured myself. The dog who had collected me and brought me in was not exactly a genius among canines, but he was no more mad, in the frightening sense, than I was. At this moment, having forgotten all about me, he was nosing among the debris, sniffing loudly, and eventually he located a dirty dish half-full of unfresh water, which he proceeded to slurp up. I, meanwhile, had taken the precaution of hiding myself under an upturned box, which had one corner propped on an old rubber boot. This lay on its side, offering me a tempting tunnel of retreat in the event of danger. Meanwhile I was not too repelled by my surroundings to want to stay around to see what would happen.

Something very soon did.

The door to the room—not the door we had come through, but one leading to the rest of the house—was thrown rudely open, making both the dog and me jump at the crash as it fell back against the wall. Heavy footsteps advanced through the room, and I could hear loud noises as objects, such as chairs, tin pails, and old bottles, were kicked out of the way. Instinctively I fled down into the boot (about the smell of which, the less said the better) and cowered there, hoping one of those clumsy kicks would not connect with my soft-covered hideout.

Instead, one of them connected with the even more vulnerable behind of my poor old enemy, the dog, who let out a yelp and scrambled into a corner, where I could hear the poor beast whimpering. I was bewildered. Why should an animal return of its own free will to a house where it was ill-treated in such a fashion? I had to learn that whereas a cat, whatever its other faults, has the self-respect to oppose or flee cruelty in human beings, a dog—so much a cat's superior in many ways—has a craven soul and will lick the very boot that kicks it. I was to be given a sickening demonstration of this revolting trait during my ever-more-unwilling stay in this hell house.

"You stupid . . . !" roared an awful voice, using a word I had (mercifully) never heard before, but was to hear frequently during the next few hours. "Leaving the . . . door open!" (Another such word. Some natural feelings for human language told me that these were words no animal should hear.) The man stamped through the room to the back door and slammed it violently shut. He had a few more choice remarks to make about dogs and drafts roaring through the . . . house, and then he started looking for a bottle that still had something in it. He opened a little door, like a cupboard, and a new horrid aroma broke out of it, of food gone bad, and then, not finding what he was looking for in there, he left it open and began filling the air with curses as he pulled the room half to pieces hunting for something to drink.

You may think no other smell could by now triumph over the ones I have already described, but poking my nose cautiously out of that filthy boot, I detected a different one, one if possible even more unpleasant to me than any of the others. It was the smell of animal fear. It was coming, of course, from the dog, which was curled, quivering, in a corner of the room behind a crate, keeping as quiet as it could to avoid drawing its master's attention to itself.

Now, it may seem odd that I could feel actual sympathy for a creature who, by common reckoning, was my natural enemy, but I couldn't help feeling sorry for the poor wretch. Fancy living in such an ugly turmoil of disorder, stench, and noise, not to mention the threats and violence. Imagine being tied —in some way I could not fathom—to an owner so unfit to have the privilege of animal companionship, especially a dog's, on which, as I knew from my boys' wistful conversations on the subject, humans place a very high value. My boys yearned for a dog of their own, and for my part I sincerely wished they had this one—at least it would be properly looked after. It hurt me to think of any animal, especially such a docile, harmless great thing as this, in the clutches of the human monster who was now slumped by the table, drinking straight from the bottle.

I decided I must try to leave the house, or at least escape from the room where this horrible human was. I did not know what was the matter with him then; I thought him mad, and getting more so by the minute, and as I've said, every creature fears madness. So, making sure his back was turned, I crept quietly out of the boot and headed toward the open door through which he had come in.

Alas! My kindly feelings toward the dog, whom I regarded as a fellow victim, had dulled my wits to the obvious fact that it had no such feelings toward me. To the dog, I was still nothing but a scuttling intruder on his premises (no doubt he'd already forgotten who'd brought me here). Perhaps he wanted to gain his master's approval, or perhaps he simply acted from instinct. Anyway, he leapt out of his corner and began to chase me.

I ran like mad. The house was in darkness, and there were obstacles everywhere. I dodged and twisted; once I had to double back straight between his legs, nearly causing him to fall flat on his face. But for all his idiocy, he knew the place better than I did, with the result that before long he had cornered me.

I faced him, sending him signals of friendship, which he was too stupid (and also too excited) to interpret. He looked for a minute as if he might be going to seize me, and in no such gentle way as before, so I bared my teeth and sent him a different signal—one of fury and defiance. He got that, all right, and backed off a trifle, but he still stood, barking mindlessly but so loudly that I couldn't hear myself think. And that was a pity, because I have never needed to think more.

My best bet would probably have been to make straight at him and dash between his legs again, but before I could gather my courage to do so, the Beast came crashing along the passage.

"What the hell are you making such a filthy racket for?" he snarled, giving the dog another blow with his boot, which sent it reeling, for all it was so big. Then a light went on.

For a second the Beast and I stared at each other. He snarled like the dog and made a clumsy dive toward me. As I broke out of my corner he actually tried to put his enormous foot on me, but I dodged and raced back toward the kitchen again, while in my ears rang his roars of surprise and rage.

"Get after it, you lazy flea-bitten mutt!" he yelled to the dog.

And would you believe it, that poor-spirited creature obeyed him!

What a chase! I ran as I had never run before, with both of them after me. Occasionally I could catch my breath by hiding under some heavy object or sprinting from one hiding place to another farther away, obliging the Beast to move things (or rather hurl them) aside—at one point I was in greater danger from flying furniture than I was from either man or dog.

But in the end one of them would always spot me or uncover me. With a howl and a volley of barks, they would be after me again.

Of course I was terrified. Yet somehow, in the very thick of my peril, I was exhilarated too. All I had ever learned or trained myself to do came to my aid now: all my climbing, diving, agility, swiftness, and cunning—not to mention sheer courage. I came to realize that, barring bad luck, the pair of them together were no match for Houdini! I would outwit them yet!

But then I made my fatal mistake.

I was searching, of course, throughout the whole chase, for a way out. And at last, when I was all but at my last gasp, I thought I'd found it. A door! And to the Outdoors, too! I knew it because of the cold air that blew through. That that air bore a smell of bad food, I had no time to notice. Of course if I hadn't been half-blind with exhaustion I would have seen what trap I was running into, but as I felt the dog's hot breath right on my back, that breath of cold air deceived me. I turned sharply toward it, leapt up a little step—and suddenly—slam! I was in darkness.

And not just darkness, but cold such as I had never experienced enveloped me. A few moments' feverish exploration was enough to teach me the ghastly truth. I was not Outdoors—far from it! I was shut into a small, dark, ice-cold box.

chapter 16

Instinct told me I must get out, and quickly, for the cold was so intense that I found myself beginning to grow weak. But for once there was no escape. My brain was active, but my body could scarcely move. Chilled to the bone, I lay on the hard icy floor of the box in the utter darkness and felt a strange darkness stealing over my mind as well.

I focused my thoughts as well as I could on the sun. How I longed for its kindly, life-giving warmth! But its image faded. No sounds came to me. The great varied world outside was shut away from me as if it didn't exist.

I had never had thoughts or ideas about death, for animals, even those clever enough to know about death and to fear it and strive to avoid it, cannot face it in their minds. But now I knew that this was death, this darkness, this silence, this mortal, blood-stilling cold.

How could a fighter, an escapologist, a genius, lose his life like this? How could I let death overtake me, lying here so patiently and helplessly, with everything fading and growing dim? Yet I had no choice. Could even my great namesake have found his way out of a prison like this? No.

It was my last conscious thought.

⊙ ⊙ ⊙

I woke up slowly. I was lying in soft, blissful warmth. There was light and there were sounds, quiet voices, soothing, anxious . . .

"Look, Mark! He's opened his eyes!"

"He's alive!"

"Oh, Houdini—"

"Mom! Houdini's alive! He's moving. . . ."

With some difficulty I focused on the faces above me. Was I dreaming? Could it be them, Mark, Adam, Guy—and now their Mother? Yes, they were all there, beaming down at me. I wouldn't like to swear to it, but I do believe the Mother had tears in her eyes.

Then the Father appeared. No tears there, you can bet, but even he sounded a bit gentler than usual when he said, "How is the little terror? Good Lord. Don't tell me he's survived even a night in a fridge! Talk about *cats* having nine lives . . ."

"Well, it wasn't a whole night, Dad. Only a couple of hours." That was Mark.

"Mr. Jenkins must have gone out early to work and seen our notice. Lucky we offered a reward; I bet he'd never have bothered to let us know otherwise!"

"Pity we had to give it to him. No need to wonder what it'll get spent on," said the Father.

"How anyone could leave a poor little creature to freeze to death—"

"He said he thought it was a rat!"

"He's not so far wrong, if you ask me." That was the Father, needless to say. But all of sudden, to my astonishment, he reached out his big hand and ran the back of one finger very lightly along my fur.

"Dad! You're stroking him!"

"You know you love him really."

"Do I," said the Father, remembering himself and withdrawing his hand hastily. "Listen, you lot. You've got him back. All right. But if he ever gets out of that cage again—"

A chorus of protest greeted this.

"Of course he won't!"

"We'll see to that!"

"We'll simply stack it with books—"

"The whole set of encyclopedias!"

"He'll never get out again, we promise!"

"And what about you? Do you promise?" said the Father, sternly, turning to his mate.

She looked very ashamed and opened her mouth. But something told me not to let her promise anything rash. I created a diversion by struggling to my feet and beginning to groom my fur. I swear it still felt cold to my tongue, though I suppose it wasn't really.

"Ah, look! He's better."

A pleasing wave of loving, encouraging sounds flowed over me. I still didn't feel myself, of course, but I must say that never, in all my very independent life, have I been so glad to belong (excuse the word, it's not really appropriate) to a family.

☉ ☉ ☉

For some time after that I was quite content with cage life. They made the most tremendous effort to make it as comfortable and pleasant for me as they could. The boys waited on me hand and foot (well, paw and paw), bringing me the most delectable tidbits to eat, lovely soft bedding, toys (well, you know, just some-

times one doesn't mind having a game)—in short, everything they could think of to make me happy and satisfied. They even bought an extension to my cage so I would not feel confined.

And while I was recovering from my awful ordeal, I was willing to accept all these kindly attentions and make the most of them. But of course, inevitably, with me being me, it couldn't last forever.

After a few days I began to feel a strange restlessness. It was not quite like my usual pre-escape restlessness. It was a definite urge. Not so much to escape, as such, but to get away by myself where nobody could look at me or disturb me, to find a private nest.

More and more strongly came the recollection of my home under the kitchen floor, before I had caused the flood. I began to long for it keenly. Every night when I woke up (which I did, these days, with greater and greater difficulty), I would struggle to get out. Often the Mother, on her way to bed, would stop by my cage, crouch down, and watch me straining my back desperately against the book-weighted roof.

"Poor Houdini," she would say tenderly. "I know. But I can't, Houdini. I really mustn't. If you're going to hibernate, you must do it in your loft. Here, I'll put your cover on." And she would drape a bit of cloth over my loft.

But that only gave me an illusion of privacy. The boys would still come along in the afternoons and wake me up and play with me. Sometimes I was so weary I could hardly open my eyes.

"Why's he so dopey these days? He used to be so lively."

"Maybe he's getting ready to sleep for the winter."

"Hamsters don't, stupid."

"How do you know?"

"It doesn't say a word about it in the book."

"They don't in captivity, but perhaps wild ones do."

I didn't know what they were talking about, and I was too sleepy to find out. I only knew I had my urge. And I had to fulfill it, soon.

It was the new extension that saved me.

Funny that I'd never thought to try all the tests on the entrance plugs in that one, which I'd exhaustively investigated in my old one. Until one day, sitting up in my loft feeling quite miserable, I happened to glance across the gap between the two cylindrical houses (they were joined at the base by a tube) and noticed something.

The water bottle in my old cage was attached by a rubber band to the ventilating bars, and its spout stuck through a little hole in the second-story plug. The weight of the bottle against the outside of the plug made it impossible to push it out, and as I've already mentioned, the one downstairs had a spring cunningly affixed, which I could never budge.

But there was no need for two water bottles, so the second-story plug in the extension hadn't got one. It had a plug, though, with a little hole in it just big enough for a spout—and no spring.

For a second after noticing this, I simply stared. Then I flashed down the two tubes, through the connecting one, up the one inside the extension, and in a twinkling I had my front teeth at work, round that tiny hole.

It was delicate work and might well have been discovered before I could have enlarged the space enough to let me out; but in bracing myself for my task I pushed hard against the plug. My muscles by now were a wonder. The inventors of the cage had not anticipated anything like them. A strong steady pressure and, with a most gratifying POP, the plug flew out. I was free!

I headed down the side of the cage, down the corridor, down the stairs, dreading all the while to find the kitchen door closed. It stood as if shut, but reaching it, I saw it was not latched. By pushing my nose firmly and steadily against its bottom corner, I gradually worked it open and slipped through.

As I crossed the familiar dark kitchen, another anxiety seized me. In repairing the leaky pipe, would they not have repaired the kitchen floor too? Would my hole be blocked? I felt I hadn't the strength to gnaw a new one. But all was again well. I flashed under the stove, and there, just as always, was the gap in the boards. My heart high with delight, I dropped through.

All was as it had been, except for the new pipe. I had, of course, not the slightest desire to gnaw that, or to do anything, indeed, which might have given away my presence. To that end, I knew, I would have to be quite silent during the day. All nest-making and storage must be carried on at night, and by day I must not so much as crack a sunflower seed.

I worked hard that night, despite my growing drowsiness. Dawn and sleep overtook me only when I had made a very passable nest out of bits of soft yellow cloth I found neatly folded in a cupboard. I had shinnied up to my cookie drawer and found a princely collection of my favorite assortments, from which I

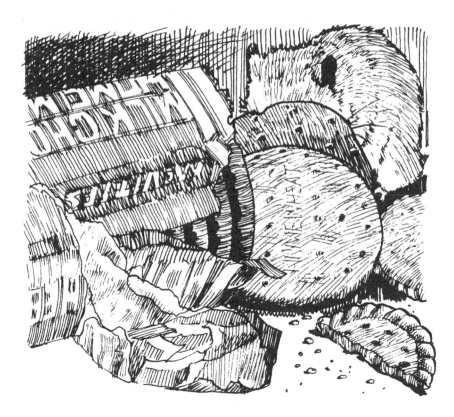

took my pick, carrying each piece carefully down, breaking it up, and storing it near my sleeping place. Knowing the tendency of cookies to go stale, I needed some seeds as well, but there would be time enough tomorrow night to run to my cage for some of those. I always kept a good supply under my mattress in the loft.

Not tonight, though. I was done in. I curled up in my cozy yellow nest. Dear Sun, I was tired! Tired but happy. Was there ever a hamster who was as happy as I was? Nor who deserved it better, I must say.

Still, I didn't sleep at once. Before dropping off, I reviewed the major triumphs of my life and, let it be added, the major downfalls. I didn't dwell on those, however. There was not one disaster, whether caused by my own fault or by sheer mischance, that I had not learned from.

After all, what else—other than survival, of course—matters?

chapter 17

I never did go up to get those seeds. I simply slept, on and on. Sometimes I would drift to the surface of consciousness and think, *I must go and get those seeds!* But I didn't really want them. I hardly seemed to get hungry at all, and if I did I would nibble a cookie, and once, on sleep-wobbly legs, I crept out and found a drink. Then I tottered back to bed like an old, old hamster.

Oh, it was so good to be private, to sleep without fear of disturbance! It was a deep prolonged sleep without dreams, indeed the "little death" the Sun had promised me, but a warm, pleasant kind, not the hideous shut-off cold one I had experienced in the fridge. In one moment of clear thought I said to myself, "If this is what death is like, I won't mind it a bit when the time comes."

But the time had not come yet!

One evening I woke up feeling completely different. Wide awake. Ready for anything. I could hear footsteps moving about overhead and smell a warm, tempting food smell, far nicer than the faded aroma of my stale store. I breathed deeply. It was stuffy under there. I sat up and scratched myself all over. Then, without a thought of danger, I dashed over to the hole and popped up under the stove.

I could see the Mother's feet standing beside it. A mischievous impulse seized me. I slipped out onto one of her shoes.

She shrieked. But then she stopped. I saw her peering down at me in total disbelief. Footsteps came running. Gently and wonderingly, she picked me up.

"Well! Look who's here!" she said.

What a welcome back I got! You'd think I'd been adventuring Outdoors again instead of just spending my winter in lazy idleness. I could tell, incidentally, that something had happened to the world outside. Even Indoors the air smelled different. Fresh. Invigorating! I wriggled in the hands that held and petted me, impatient to be allowed to run. . . .

But it was not to be, not just yet. Having exclaimed endlessly over the miracle of my return "from the dead" (it seems they all thought I had somehow got out of the house and perished), they had plans for me.

"We must take him to see his children!"

My what? I must say for all my worldly knowledge I couldn't imagine what this could mean. But I was soon to learn.

Chattering gaily, the boys (all of whom seemed to have grown enormously since I had last seen them) put me into a ventilated box and carried me some distance through the street. I knew it by the smells and sounds that came through the airholes. Most of the sounds were birdsong, and very pretty too. Then we were indoors again and I recognized Ben's voice.

"Don't tell me the little twerp showed up again after all this time!"

"We think he's been hibernating under our kitchen floor. But he hasn't done any damage, so even Dad's not too annoyed."

"Can he see the babies?"

"They're not such babies anymore, but bring him up."

I must admit to being very curious by now. Babies?

The lid of the box came off. I reared up and put my front paws on the rim, looking over. And what a sight met my eyes.

There, just below, was Oggi, in her cage, but with the top open, so that I had a bird's-eye view. She looked sleek and contented. Around her were a number of different-colored balls of fur. Two of them were spotted, like her. One was dark, almost black. And three were golden. Like me!

Ben reached his finger down and stirred the clump of fur.

"Wake up, you lot! Your dad's come to see you."

They twitched a bit and several little hamster faces were raised. I could only gaze.

"Shall we put him in with them?" asked Adam.

But Ben shook his head. "Better not. They're funny little beasts. You never know, he might hurt them."

Hurt them? Not me! Another male hamster might perhaps— a primitive who did not know his own kind or grasp the wonderful processes of nature. But I knew now. These were my offspring, mine and Oggi's. I wouldn't have hurt them for the world.

But on the other hand, I was not sorry not to be put among them. I felt very strange, looking at them. Overwhelmed. There are some feelings that are too big for small creatures, even highly intelligent ones. I sent Oggi a rather incoherent signal of praise, which I don't think she noticed, and dropped back with a sense of relief into the box. I knew I had survived another of life's high spots, but for once, I didn't know how to take it. I am,

if the truth be told, really better fitted for the physical than the emotional trials of this life.

And that nearly brings me to the end of my story so far. I say so far because I'm not finished yet, by a long way. I'm not even slowing down. Well, not noticeably, anyway.

As I said to begin with, I have the run of the house now, more or less. Oh, sometimes they shut me up in the cage, but what's the use? I can usually get out again. All the plugs have worked loose now and they can't lean heavy objects against all of them. Anyway, now that I'm older, I no longer gnaw on anything except the blocks of wood they provide for the purpose, so even the Father has come round to me. I ran up his trouser leg the other night by mistake (I thought for a moment he was Mark, who's now almost the same size) and he just laughed and called me a little devil.

I've been allowed to keep my nest under the floor. When no more flooding occurred, they decided it wasn't worth the fuss of tearing up the floorboards again.

My piano is still available to me, and in it I keep myself in condition. The temptation here, to chew the felts and make a nest, is perhaps the greatest I have to subdue. But I do subdue it.

You see, I have arrived at a way of life with my family. They have given way, and I have given way. Compromise. That's the secret of humans and animals living contentedly together. Humans and humans too, no doubt. Forgive me for ending on a preachy note. But as I get older, I find myself becoming less of an adventurer, more of a philosopher.

Perhaps that's how it goes, for all of us who are born with quite *exceptional* talents.

About the Author

Lynne Reid Banks was born in London in 1929 and spent World War II on the Canadian prairies as a "war guest." On returning home, she studied drama and acted for five years. She then went into journalism, becoming the first woman TV news reporter in Britain in 1955. In 1960 her first novel, *The L-Shaped Room*, was published, and it was later filmed. In 1962 she emigrated to Israel, where she married, had three sons, and spent eight years living on a kibbutz and teaching English. She returned to London with her family in 1971 and since then has written nearly forty books, mainly novels for adults and young readers, including the award-winning Indian in the Cupboard series; the two Harry the Poisonous Centipede books; *I, Houdini; The Farthest-Away Mountain;* and *The Fairy Rebel.* Her latest novel is *The Dungeon.* She lives in a three-hundred-year-old farmhouse in Dorset, England, with her husband. She often travels and visits schools at home and abroad.